"I love Laura's books. They evoke the true ineffable charm and mystery that is the heart and soul of New Orleans."
- Bryan Batt

"Whether you've been there or not, Laura Cayouette brings New Orleans to life. Her Charlotte Reade character isn't just great at unraveling mysteries, she's a terrific guide through the music, food and culture of the city."
- Allison Leotta

"This book is a trip to New Orleans--not a tourist trip, but an intimate journey to the heart of the city and its colorful, exuberant people. If you love NOLA, this is the book for you. If you don't know NOLA, this book will make it come alive for you, and you will fall in love. The setting is vivid and wondrously wrought, and it's just the beginning. The novel brims with interesting characters and an engaging mystery to boot. I highly recommend this book."
- Jennifer Kincheloe

"New Orleans is comprised of equal parts interesting people, great food, beauty, darkness, and mystery; all of which are held together with a dash of magic. Laura Cayoutte has used this same recipe to craft her latest book."
-Jon McCarthy

LEMONADE FARM

"I've read Laura's novel *Lemonade Farm* and can attest to its power. It evokes the 1970s in a painfully accurate way, and is beautifully written. She manages a wide cast of characters and somehow paints adults, teenagers and children with equal skill without ever condescending to any of them. Her skill at characterization and turns of phrase, coupled with a great sense of place, makes this a heck of a novel."
-Tom Franklin

KNOW SMALL PARTS:
AN ACTOR'S GUIDE TO TURNING MINUTES INTO MOMENTS AND MOMENTS INTO A CAREER

"Laura's outward beauty could have guaranteed her much more in this business perhaps even worldwide fame. She could have taken an easier route for her professional pursuits but instead chose to make it about the work and only the work. She is a role model in that regard and a true leading lady. Enjoy what she has to say and see if you can see yourself in her journey. She still has some big important parts to play."
-Kevin Costner

"She's nailed the daily life of an actor in L.A. about as perfectly detailed as it gets... You can say that Laura is amazingly correct in everything she says and sees, but she makes you hunt for the urgent need to do it which is at the bottom of all."
-Richard Dreyfuss

"Laura Cayouette is a working actress that also has a happy, well-balanced life. Figuring out how she manages this feat is certainly worth a read."
-Reginald Hudlin

"Anyone who has met Laura knows that she is unforgettable. Perhaps even more impressive is that she has found a way to translate this personal charisma and life-force into her appearances on screen, making the most of every second of camera time given to her. She has literally figured out a way to bottle lightning. I'm sure that her observations and guidance will be invaluable to the actor who is looking to make his or her mark in the film world and to build a career, moment by moment."
-Lou Diamond Phillips

PREFACE

In an effort to capture the unique culture of New Orleans, many of the people and places mentioned in this fictional novel exist in reality. As such, you can trace Charlotte Reade's steps and enjoy many of her experiences for yourself. In an effort to entertain, I've sometimes bent these real people and places to my fictional will so "real life" experiences may differ.

I have included an Appendix listing many of the restaurants, tours, people and events mentioned in this novel along with links to their sites. For more information and photos on anything mentioned in this book, use the search tool in LAtoNOLA (latonola.com), the blog upon which many of the book's recollections are based.

I've also built a playlist of music videos and videos of parades and other events, places and people included in this story on my YouTube channel:
https://www.youtube.com/user/latonolawordpress

You can link directly to the playlist at:
https://www.youtube.com/playlist?list=PL-T9AQ-VvsW2wQ__ObsptNU-G6g7yJIb7

And I've created a clipboard of photos on Pinterest:
https://www.pinterest.com/latonola/

Enjoy!

FAMILY TREES

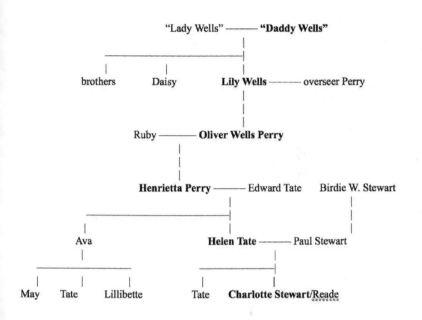

"Lady Wells" ———— **"Daddy Wells"**

brothers   Daisy   **Lily Wells** ———— overseer Perry

Ruby ———— **Oliver Wells Perry**

Henrietta Perry ———— Edward Tate   Birdie W. Stewart

Ava   **Helen Tate** ———— Paul Stewart

May   Tate   Lillibette   Tate   **Charlotte Stewart/Reade**

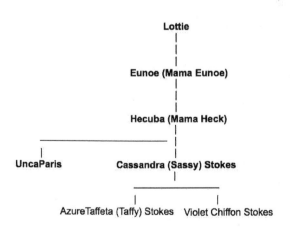

Lottie

Eunoe (Mama Eunoe)

Hecuba (Mama Heck)

UncaParis   **Cassandra (Sassy) Stokes**

AzureTaffeta (Taffy) Stokes   Violet Chiffon Stokes

Special Thanks
to
Kat Ford
Danielle Tanguis
and
Tracy Norwood
Adam Stevenson
Wendy Talley

For "The Three Wise Men."
Quentin who told me to write it,
Ted who read every page as I wrote it
and Andy who supported me all along the way.
Thank you.

LA to NOLA Press

© 2018 Laura Cayouette

ISBN-13: 978-1717227515
ISBN-10: 1717227511

First Edition: March 2018

Back cover photo by Robert Larriviere

Many of the people and places mentioned in this fictional novel exist in
"real life." At times, the author has bent these real people and places to
her fictional will. Although the author has made every effort to ensure
the accuracy and completeness of much of the information contained in
this book, we assume no responsibility for errors, inaccuracies,
omissions, or any inconsistency herein. Any slights of people, places,
or organizations are unintentional.

THE HAUNTED HEIRLOOM
A Charlotte Reade Mystery

Laura Cayouette

To JAYNE –
My BIGGEST FAN IN
SEATTLE !

Lana Cayouette

Chapter 1

The photographer set lights on a white seamless backdrop while three people worked on me. I held up another hot-roller setting pin while the hair person protected the top of my ear with a folded piece of toilet tissue. Her face looked determined as she wound a strawberry blonde lock around another heated barrel and pinned it in place. The stylist clasped a necklace behind me and came around to see if it passed muster. I shut my eyes as the makeup person came at me with an eyeshadow brush. Air-conditioned fingers unclasped the necklace at the nape of my neck and disappeared.

"Open." Makeup artists' voices always went up at the end when they gave this instruction, almost like it was a question. I stared into her caramel eyes. She took me in like a canvas and reached for her eyeshadow palette. "So what was it like to work with Clarence Pool? Does everybody ask you that? They do, right?"

Dane looked up from the refreshment table. "Don't answer that. Save it for the interview."

I smiled at the makeup artist. "Sorry." I closed my eyes again as she selected a deeper shade of brown for contour. "It was amazing."

"Yeah, I figured. Gotta be, right? I seen every one a his movies a buncha times. He's what's up."

He was. *7 Sisters* was actually the second movie Clarence had cast me in, but "Charlie" was written with me in mind. It still blew me away that I'd inspired this legendary man who'd inspired so many. I had grown used to hanging out with Clarence — playing board games, watching movies, talking movies and making the most of L.A. life. Working together was an anomaly, a side-dish to our friendship. But I wasn't so blasé that I didn't realize what a rare honor it was to be in his next big release.

When the hair person finished with the top roller, she grabbed a hair dryer and waved cool air over the lower rollers. "Gotta move fast. Am I bothering you?" She wasn't talking to me.

The makeup person gestured with an eyebrow pencil. "I'm fine until mascara."

Dane pushed thick brown waves from his eye. "Do you mind if we start now? We probably won't get into anything, just the preliminaries. Cool?"

I looked his way without moving my face. "Yeah, that's fine."

He grabbed a pocket recorder, a pad and pen and pulled a foldout chair to my side. "Can we not do the blow drying for a minute?"

The hair person pressed her hand to the bottom rollers, then the top. "Yeah, I'm good." She handed me the box of bobby pins and released one of the bottom rollers. Dane turned on the recorder as she rolled the hair like a lasso and pinned it to my head.

"Okay, so we're here with Charlotte Reade, star of the upcoming Clarence Pool movie, *7 Sisters*."

I laughed. "I wouldn't go that far. There's a lot of stars in that movie. I'm more star-adjacent."

2

"But you're one of the sisters."

"Yes. The seven of us, including Oscar and Golden Globe winners. And there's all the men too."

"Let's start with how you came to New Orleans. You moved here in 2009?"

"When the Saints were on their way to the Super Bowl. Timing is everything and mine was perfect. Who Dat!"

"Who Dat!"

I laughed, trying not to move. "It was actually a funeral that brought me from L.A. to New Orleans. Sassy, the woman who'd raised three generations of my family."

"I'm sorry for your loss."

"Thank you." I was still getting used to people being so kind and polite. "I mean, I always knew I would move here when I retired, but arriving at that moment in this city's history was just... I couldn't leave after I realized how happy I was capable of being in this place. Now. Not when it made sense for some other reason."

The photographer announced, "Ready."

Dane smiled and snapped off the recorder then turned to the photographer. "Great. Thank you. Ladies, how long?"

Everyone examined me like I was something they were taking a test on, then assessed. Hair was almost done, just needed to spray when makeup could give her a minute. Makeup needed five. The stylist shrugged and said, "I can't start until they finish."

I chimed in. "I did ten years of runway. I can do two minute changes."

Dane waved his hand. "Let's keep this train rollin'." He clicked the recorder on again. "Yes, right. So, you came for a funeral and stayed for the Saints."

I laughed. "Pretty much." My smile steadied and went wide for the application of lip liner.

Dane asked about what it was like to work with megastars like Graham Paisley and Madison Frye. And what it was like to work with Clarence, of course. I'd already done a few interviews focusing on *7 Sisters* and was used to having ready answers for those type of questions. But interviews in Louisiana were sometimes different. People cared about different things here. Most wanted to know what it was like to work with our local crew and facilities. Some asked things like, "What's the best part of your job?," "What are the non-artistic influences in your career?" or "What's the last thing that made you smile?" No one ever asked that in L.A. It's a fairly revealing question, one worth asking.

We stopped when it came time for me to change. I always felt a little nervous before a shoot and it'd been a long time since I was a model. I was good at a lot of things, but I knew my weaknesses and I'd never been the world's best print model. I came alive on the runway and had a strong walk, but I'd long ago gotten used to the idea that I'd never set the magazine world on fire with a distant stare and a strategically-slung hip.

As my heels clicked onto the seamless, I turned and closed my eyes then took a deep breath. Patrick's voice from dinner last night popped into my head. "You're being ridiculous. You're used to comparing yourself with Kate Moss. Around here, they're used to taking pictures of the King of Bacchus, the mayor, trombonists, people who've never modeled."

I stretched my face three times, opened my eyes and smiled slowly. Very slowly. I heard the clicking of approval. I let random images pass through my head. Sweet olive blossoms. Their honeyed perfume filled my senses and I genuflected. A parade got a short laugh and an open-mouthed smile. Then I pictured Wonder Woman and my body shifted with strength as my expression grew steely. Patrick was right. I wasn't the world's greatest model, but I knew what I was doing. I was a pro. It was time I let myself own what I was, instead of owning what I wasn't.

I wasn't a star. I didn't have gold statues. But I'd worked surrounded by people who had shelves full of them since my very first film twenty years ago – in a part that was written for me. My career wasn't what I'd pictured when I was studying Shakespeare and Ibsen in New York, but it had paid my bills and given me an opportunity to contribute to some unforgettable movies and TV shows. In L.A., I was a "working actor," someone who could support themselves through acting. I was in the same one percent of our industry as Tom Cruise and Leonardo DiCaprio, but I was scraping the bottom of that graph.

In New Orleans, I was one of the rare few who could support themselves as an actor. In audition waiting rooms in L.A., the working actors mostly knew each other. We knew who to fear. Almost from the beginning of my career in New Orleans, people seemed to know who I was even if I didn't introduce myself. A few of them told me they loved my work in something.

I'd felt respected for my work in L.A. and got plenty of compliments, but here I sporadically felt admired. Like I was a star. It could be disheartening at times. It could feel like the person was creating distance between us, making me better than them somehow. I'd seen that a lot when I'd hung out with my fancier L.A. friends and knew it wasn't the way I wanted to experience people. But, it did feel nice to be appreciated for contributing to people's entertainment. Though I'd never wanted to be paparazzi-famous after seeing what my celebrity friends' lives were like, I'd always been willing to be known for doing good work. Maybe even admired.

I was looking forward to Patrick getting home from the gym so I could tell him how he'd helped me at the photo shoot. I tried to never take his support for granted after so many years of doing life on my own. I'd even had guys interfere with my career, sabotage me. Patrick had no use for the spotlight but fully supported my kooky job that included strange hours, occasional travel and sometimes kissing other men. He was a keeper.

I hung my rubber Oka-B. sandals on the rack behind our bedroom door. Sassy's chandelier was behaving itself. What I'd come to think of as the spirit of Sassy's mother, Mama Heck, had been quiet lately. Patrick still hadn't seen the chandelier move. He'd settled into an attitude of loving me despite my believing in a haunted chandelier that never did anything other than light the room. I wasn't sure how to feel about his willingness to love me past what he was certain was some sort of detachment from reality.

The red digital number on the answering machine blinked. I had to be one of the few people left in the country still using a home phone and machine. I'd long ago forgotten the code to check messages remotely.

My brother coughed. "Hey." Another cough. Maybe the sound of sipping water. "Hey Charlotte, it's Tate. I have interesting news. Call me."

Interesting? That didn't sound like a pregnancy announcement or someone getting hurt. Interesting.

Tate picked up on the third ring. "Hey! I was hoping that was you. I'm waiting on an email and I can't move forward until I get it, so we have a minute."

I jumped right in. "What's interesting?"

"So I'd been doing the ancestry thing online and then I stopped, right?"

"Yeah."

He fidgeted with some papers. "Before I quit doing it, I went back a lot of generations on Dad's side. I got confused for a while because there was another Stewart family that settled in Delaware. Ours is the Massachusetts Stewarts."

I wasn't sure where this was going but I was intrigued. "I sorta remember you telling me something about this."

"Right. So before I cut off my account, there was a woman I exchanged emails with. We thought we were related but she turned out to be a Delaware Stewart."

"Okay." I was already getting impatient. There was nothing particularly irritating about my brother except that he was my little brother. I hoped I was going to agree that this story was "interesting." I started pacing the living room.

"She emailed me a few weeks ago and said she'd bought a book from someone online. It was a Stewart family journal from the turn of the century. After she'd looked at it a while, she realized it was our family's journal."

"Oh wow." Definitely interesting.

"So, she found my email and asked if I wanted to buy it for what she paid."

"Which was?"

He chuckled. "Fifty dollars. And don't give me a hard time about not wanting to pay for the ancestry thing because this is way more worth it. I'm emailing you a few photos. And Charlotte..." His pause was dramatic, nearly theatrical. Or maybe it was normal and I was looking at him like a big sister again. Our forties seemed a bit old for us to still play those roles, but it was habitual. "There's a family tree."

"Yes!" I jumped. "Does it have Birdie on it?" Birdie was our grandmother, Dad's mom. We'd been searching for her maiden name for nearly a year. It seemed strange that her own children didn't know Birdie's full name, but we'd grown to accept it as lost in the record. Turns out, there was a time when it wasn't uncommon for there to be no record of a woman's maiden name. Her identity was as her husband's wife, not an individual partnering with another individual.

"No, but wait. I'm telling you. So, the woman. Susan is her name. Susan is the one who made the family tree. She was looking through everything in the journal and realized there were births and deaths listed throughout so she started making the tree."

"This is so cool."

"Yes, but she stops when she realizes it's definitely the wrong tree. It took a while because there were actually a lot of names that lined up. A lot of her tree had common names like James and William and ours does too, so she got through a lot of the journal before she was sure. Then she emailed me. So I've had the journal for about a week, getting to it when I can. And every time I get to a wedding, death or birth, I check it against the tree. And I have to say that it was really neat watching all of these branches on the tree filled in with people I was reading about. And written by them. Our family. It's pretty great. I'm glad I went on that site. And I'm glad I reached out to Susan. That really paid off. I wasn't even thinking something like this."

I was getting antsy. "So tell me about the tree!"

"Right. So at some point I'm past where she stopped only I don't know that yet. Then I see this name."

Finally.

Tate took a breath. "I thought about what you said about Aunt Carol saying Birdie's name was like her father's."

"Tate, what is the name?"

"So I see the name Bird. Leonard Bird Wells."

"Leonard Bird Wells? So Birdie W. Stewart was Birdie Wells Stewart? Seriously? That's weird.

Mom's family tree had Wells in it. All those relatives from Wells Plantation."

"Wells was a really common name. It's like the Stewart thing. The more common your last name is, the harder it can be to tell which family is yours."

The tinkling of the chandelier crystals rattled down the long hallway. I wasn't surprised. Mama Heck's spirit always seemed to react to talk of family. Patrick's car alarm honked outside as he armed it.

"Patrick's home. I gotta go."

"Okay. Take a look at those photos when you get a minute."

"Definitely."

I trotted down the hall and peeked into the bedroom. The chandelier was settling into stagnancy. Dang. The door opened and Patrick gave me a quick hug before putting his gym bag and *7 Sisters* briefcase down, one of my gifts from the production. I didn't bother mentioning that he'd missed the chandelier acting up again.

"Last night I made a big bowl of that chilled orzo dish you like."

"Yes!"

I laughed. "So dinner's ready whenever you're hungry."

He kissed me. "Best day ever."

"You always say that."

He shrugged. "It's always true."

I decided not to question it, to just relax and enjoy that he was in a good mood and liked my cooking. My new life was constantly testing my ability to just relax and enjoy.   ·

While Patrick washed up, I downloaded Tate's photos and opened them. The book was covered in hand-tooled leather. There were a few photos of yellowed pages with splotched-ink cursive lists and anecdotes.

The last photo was Susan's family tree. The final names were written in my brother's sloppy script. Leonard Bird Wells and Daisy Wells. I stared at the name a moment, my breath catching. Daisy Wells? The two daughters from the Wells Plantation were Lily, my great-great-grandmother, and her younger sister Daisy. Maybe Birdie wasn't lying about her mother being the daughter of a wealthy plantation owner. Maybe my paternal great-grandmother was the daughter of my maternal great-great-grand aunt.

Logic caught up to me quickly and I chuckled to myself. Daisy Wells would have been her maiden name. The Daisy Wells in Tate's book would've been Mrs. Leonard Bird Wells. I shut my laptop and headed to the kitchen cabinet for plates.

Chapter 2

I still miscalculated sometimes. I was so used to L.A. traffic that I could still arrive at an appointment up to forty minutes too early. This was one of those times. Luckily, my audition was in the French Quarter so I wandered down Royal Street, staring into windows displaying paintings, antiques, jewelry and Civil War artifacts.

As I passed M.S. Rau Antiques, I remembered my niece Julia saying I should ask the guy there if he'd go with me to May Baily's Place and look at the flask in their display case. I felt silly asking. I'd found the flask when I was on a tour of "Brothels, Bordellos and Ladies of the Night." The symbol of a well pump was imprinted on the bottom of the silver flask. It was the same symbol I'd seen on the top of Sassy's chandelier before we hung it. Though we couldn't figure out what the symbol was at the time, it was the tour guide, Christine Miller, who suggested it was the mark of a plantation.

When I found the same symbol imprinted in a wax seal at Bryan Batt's shop, theory became fact. The wax seal had closed a bill of sale for a slave named Lottie from the Wells Plantation. It had been signed by Leonard Percy or Perry or something. Leonard must've been another of those fairly common names.

Julia, my mother and I had met Ludovic when we wandered into M.S. Rau during their visit shortly after my move. He gave us a personal tour of the shop full of exotic collectibles and furnishings. The store had secret doorways and chambers containing everything from an art gallery featuring Monet and Renoir to a room of million-dollar clocks and self-playing instruments.

I nodded to the security guard as I headed for the jewelry counter. The pearl-like strands of opals shot red, violet and green fire at me as elaborate diamond earrings glinted nearby. But no sign of Ludovic. I wandered past cabinets of silver tableware and remembered the desk area toward the back of the room, before the small staircase leading to sculptures and storied ornamentals.

Over the bar-like wall, I could see the jet black hair of a woman flipping through a stack of papers. I hoped she wasn't counting. "Excuse me. Is Ludovic working today?"

"No, not today." She stopped flipping papers and turned to me, looking out from under thick Bettie-Page-like bangs. Her eyebrows were equally dramatic as were her bright red lips. Her face went wide with recognition. "Hey, aren't you Christine's friend?"

I wasn't sure I could get away with calling Christine Miller a friend. I wouldn't ask her for a ride to the airport. But, I knew what she meant. "Yes, we met at a food booth. You're a Pussyfooter, right?"

"Yeah. Caroline. I heard you got in. Welcome! You dancing in Festigals?"

I'd been in love with the Pussyfooters since the first time I saw the pink army of women-over-thirty dancing down St. Charles during the Super Bowl Mardi Gras. I loved their burlesque-inspired uniforms of pink wigs, corsets and fishnets with white combat boots. It was the perfect expression of the woman I'd wanted to become when I moved here – someone strong, not tough. Someone who could embrace her inner pink.

It had never really occurred to me that I could be a part of the parades. My second year here I was super-excited just to be able to wave at people I knew when they marched past. Sometimes I even got a hug from some new acquaintance. I'd grown used to standing beside famous people over the years, but I got a thrill from being associated with the people who made Carnival happen. Growing up, I'd never realized that the people in the floats pay for everything from the beads and toys they throw to the police and clean-up. Mardi Gras was a community event as much as it was the "biggest free party in the world." For me, becoming a Pussyfooter meant I was now officially part of the community.

Membership was by invitation. A Pussyfooter who'd met all of her obligations for the year could enter one name in the lottery and hope there were enough slots for their choice to be included. I'd met Sabine the same day Christine introduced me to Caroline. She was a doctor of internal medicine at the local hospital and a huge fan of my blog, LAtoNOLA.

We'd run into each other at a festival months later and she invited me to lunch to tell me about the organization and it's obligations and ask me about myself. When she walked away, Patrick seemed so impressed that I started to realize this was a fairly big deal. The Pussyfooters were literally a group of the city's movers and shakers.

The lunch with Sabine was part job interview, part sales pitch, part warning. Though many dance krewes had popped up since the Pussyfooters started the trend in 2001, most were not year-round obligations with around fifty non-profit events and a giant Mardi Gras ball to raise funds for those affected by domestic violence. And Sabine had a cousin and a coworker who'd been hounding her for the invite – she felt she had to consider them.

I'd spent most of my life terrified of large groups of women. Despite being a legacy, I'd never even looked into sororities. I'd been a gymnast, a model and an actor – all activities where you could win as a team but competed individually. As Sabine spelled out the rehearsal schedule and dues, I felt excited and started really hoping Sabine picked me over her cousin and coworker, and that I made it through the lottery. I finally felt ready to be part of a large group of women. I'd gotten Sabine's congratulatory call a few weeks ago and jumped and squealed like a teenager. Patrick was so excited, he took me on a low-budget shopping spree for pink bling to wear with my future uniform.

Festigals would be my first time parading with the group. It was just a second line through the French Quarter, so we didn't have to know the dances yet or even have our official uniforms. Sabine had loaned me a pink wig and one of her older corsets and I'd bought my boots online the day I became a "Kitten." The parade was part of a women's networking and empowerment weekend benefitting breast cancer and other female-centric non-profits.

"Yeah. I'm nervous. It's my first time dancing in a parade."

Caroline stood from her rolling chair and rested her arms on the wall between us. "Don't worry. You don't have to know anything for this. Just have fun. Seriously, you'll be having to memorize eight new dances soon enough. And at least one performance dance. Enjoy this. It'll be fun. What'd you need Ludo for?"

"Right. Um, I was going to ask him for a favor."

Caroline smiled. "Anything I can do?"

I smiled back. "Maybe. I'm not sure anyone can help but my niece thought it was worth a shot. There's a flask at May Baily's that's stamped with my family's symbol. It's a pump, like for a well. Wells Plantation. Anyway, I was just wondering if someone who knew a little about antiques could take a look at it and see if there was anything interesting about it."

"Interesting?"

"Like, maybe you could tell something about it by lookin' at it that I just wouldn't know."

She handed me a card from a silver holder near her elbow. "I'll do it. I know a lot about antiques. We all do. But, I'm happy to do it."

I looked to the card. Caroline Bozier. Then back to her smile. "Thanks. Tell Ludovic I said hey."

I'd never been in a sorority, but maybe this was what it felt like to have insta-sisters. I was still feeling the pink high of being a Pussyfooter when I fell in behind a group of slow moving tourists on Royal. They wove and wandered, taking up the whole street. As I closed in looking for a hole to pass through, I heard them chatting.

"Look at this street. What a disaster."

"I would never drive my car down this mess."

I could see the hump running down the center of the road like the spine of a whale, but it was freshly repaired and paved. Not a pothole in sight. It might've been the only street in the city you could say that about. So, I exploded. "This is the nicest street in our whole city. This place is older than America so maybe streets aren't our best thing, but there ain't a dang thing wrong with this street."

I burst through them and strutted down the humped, pothole-free street. I had a lot of patience for tourists but I'd grown even more fiercely protective of the city since moving here. Katrina made me realize how dangerous it was to take this place for granted, but living here had pulled me deep into love of the culture and beauty of this wonky world. My heart was finally home and I couldn't abide insults to my home.

The waiting room was empty. I signed in and was called before I could even sit. I wasn't crazy about the part of the lead's mother in a teen-scream TV movie, but I'd had to grow less picky after moving to New Orleans. In L.A., half my income came from commercials. Very few commercials shot in Louisiana. Even fewer that were union and for national usage. I was used to doing two to five national commercials a year. That gave me the freedom to turn down a lot of TV and film parts I found unpalatable for whatever reason. I could even turn down commercials for any product I found offensive and still stay afloat. Integrity was expensive but I slept well.

Moving to a secondary market meant being cut out of most casting. By the time a project came to Louisiana, the leads had already been cast. Maybe even most of the supporting parts. That often left small roles in projects I might not like, playing parts I wasn't crazy about. "Janet," the lead's mother in a teen-scream TV movie, was one of those parts. But I did my best.

I pulled my two-seater convertible to the curb in front of the home my family had built when they arrived in New Orleans some time after the Civil War. Cousin May had done a nice job turning it into three units when my family left the city after The Storm. A walking tour of about a dozen tourists was gathered across the street as I retrieved my shoulder bag from the trunk. I lingered, listening in.

A tourist in a bright red "I put ketchup on my ketchup" t-shirt gestured toward Jason's Unit 3 window in the front of the house. "People live here?"

The guide smiled. "Yes, it's a neighborhood."

"They live with ghosts? In haunted houses?"

The guide laughed. "Anyone living in New Orleans is probably living in a haunted house." He motioned with a paper fan. "This way."

I closed my trunk and hurried to him. "Hey, excuse me."

The guide turned. "Yes?"

I pointed across the street. "Did you just tell a story about that house?"

"Yes, ma'am."

"Do you mind if I ask what it is?"

He chuckled. "Pay the fare like the rest, lady." Then he walked away.

I wasn't sure Jason would be home yet but it was worth a try, so before turning my door key I tapped on his door next to me.

Jason was wearing seersucker shorts and nothing else when he pulled the door open. "Oh hey Charlotte."

"Hey. Sorry to bother, but remember a couple years back you said you took that tour of our neighborhood? The one where they told about the chandelier?"

"Yeah, sure. But it was more like four years ago, the tour." He gestured for me to come in and headed to the fireplace mantle for a koozie-clad High Life. "Want one?"

I stayed near the doorway. "Naw, I'm good. Do you know the name of that tour? And even better, do you know the guide's name?"

Jason took a swig and wiped his lips with the back of his hand. "Not off the top of my head, but I could probably find it out for ya. Fun factoid about the boy next door, I'm quite the accountant so I hang on to all my receipts. Got 'em sorted in boxes by year and category."

"Great. Perfect."

"Yeah, I'll dig it out and email you later."

"That'd be great. Thank you so much. Hopefully it has the guide's name on it."

"I'm sure I've got it written down somewhere if it's not there. They only know what they're told, you know. The guides. They have a script so it probably doesn't matter which guide you pick as long as it's the same company."

"Yeah, maybe. Thanks again."

The phone started ringing as I headed down the long hallway to our living room at the back of the house. I grabbed it just before the machine picked up and was excited when I saw the name on the cordless. "Sofia!"

"Hi. I finally had a minute so I thought I'd give it a try. Are you busy?"

"I just walked in but I'm good. Man, it's been too long."

Sofia and I met in high school. Over the years, there'd been chunks of time where we fell out of touch. We went years without talking or writing when she moved oversees. But every time we reconnected, it was like we'd never skipped a beat. It had been a just-add-water friendship from the minute we realized we'd worn matching striped v-neck shirts the day we met. I'd already been in L.A. for nearly a decade when Sofia and her sister moved there. It meant so much having friends who weren't interested in passing a script to one of my fancier friends. Having lived outside the country for nearly twenty years, Sofia didn't even know who most of them were.

"I know. I've just been really busy with Nia and the business. Mark's on the road with his sculptures again. Ever since that *Sex and the City* episode where they showed his piece, it's been crazy."

"That's good though."

"It is good. It wasn't even his best piece. I feel like a single mom lately, but it's good. Mark deserves it. Better late than never and he worked a long time for this."

I smiled. "You deserve a vacation. You should come visit. You make it all work for Mark, you should get a reward now that it's going well."

Sofia giggled. "I did. Last year was redoing the yard. This year I'm doing a makeover. I joined a pilates gym, dropped way too much money on a shag haircut that's so cute. You have to see it. I'll send a picture."

"You'll forget. Write it down." Though Sofia was a few years younger, we were both getting to that age where it was easier to forget things than remember them. It was like our brains had reached maximum capacity around thirty-five and were now dumping information to make room for new.

"And I bought a whole new wardrobe. You'd love it. Stuff to show off my new and improved pilates body. Cute stuff."

I tried not to be disappointed that she'd spent her windfall on anything other than a trip to visit me. I'd gone back to L.A. a few times already. It was getting harder to explain this place and why I was so happy here. I needed Sofia to experience it for herself. But I was glad she was doing nice things for herself after all the weight she'd been carrying. "Send me photos. I wanna see."

"What about you? Did you meet those pink ladies yet?"

"I'll be meeting a bunch of them at the parade next week. I ran into one today though, a woman I met once before at a festival food booth. She said she's gonna come with me to see the flask at that bar that used to be a brothel back in the Storyville days."

"I'm really glad you're doing that whole dancer thing. Unless it was for showbiz stuff, you became such a homebody in L.A. Now, you're always out doing something."

"Except going to movies. I hardly ever go to movies in a theatre anymore. And I don't even really miss it. Which is crazy 'cause I went at least once a week for year after year."

Sofia snickered. "It was your painkiller. Now, you don't need to escape."

I chuckled. "It's true."

She laughed. "Plus movies suck lately."

I laughed too. "Also true. Sad, but true."

"And Patrick is good?"

I smiled hard. "So good." Sofia had been there for me through many confounding and lonely years in L.A. but she never lost the faith that I'd meet a guy someday who'd make the whole thing worth it. "You have to meet him."

"I know. I will." Sofia switched ears, the microphone scratching against her new shag haircut. "You think you guys will get married?"

I thought about being coy, not jinxing things, holding back – but Sofia was one of the few people I could tell anything. "I do. I hope so anyway. I' mean, I'm scared. It didn't go so well the first time."

Sofia laughed. "We all got married before the ink on our college degrees dried. At least you got two degrees first, but we were all really young. You were like a whole other woman from now. And I'm pretty sure Patrick's a completely different human than your ex."

I laughed.

Sofia started chewing something. "I'm going to keep saying it until you hear it. Wait until there's an actual problem before you start spinning over something."

I laughed. "I know, I know. I've been doing that. I'm gettin' better at it. Any muscle you exercise gets stronger and for years I exercised the muscle of worrying about things to feel in control. I've been exercising the muscle of letting life unfold at it's own pace here and, like you said, tryin' not to worry until there's an actual problem. But that other muscle still pops up on occasion. It was pretty freaking strong by the time I left L.A."

Sofia got serious. "Yeah, but like, really leave here. Quit letting this place affect you. You survived. You're safe now."

I sighed. "It really is like that, isn't it? That place did some damage. Emotional scar tissue."

"Yeah, but just let it go. Just like, say, 'Seeya' and be done."

I laughed. "Oh, okay. I'll just stop."

Sofia laughed. "Yeah."

I looked out the window at the blooming magnolia tree towering over the house. "Okay."

Chapter 3

I wandered the Garden District Book Shop waiting for the tour to start. I'd gone by the store often enough that I was learning the staff's names. The gentle-faced man who'd led me to clues for finding Taffy and Chiffon's birth mother was Ted. The petite woman with a halo of red curls was named Amy. I still didn't know purple-hair woman's name but I liked all of her funky glasses, especially the green ones with the tiny white polkadots.

Ted smiled and waved me over to where he was packaging a signed book to be mailed out. "Hey. More research?"

I laughed as I neared a pile of boxes and envelopes. "I'm going on a tour."

Ted's turn to laugh. "Of your own neighborhood?" Before I could explain myself he added, "That could be cool. Tell me if you learn anything interesting."

"I'm not optimistic. It's a ghost tour. Not really my thing."

He pulled the strip off the sticky seal and pressed the large envelope closed. "Don't believe in ghosts?"

I wasn't sure how to answer that. A lot of the stories I'd heard and reality shows I'd seen stretched credulity. But I'd been living with a chandelier that moved in ways I couldn't explain. I couldn't unsee the things I'd seen so, yeah, I guess I did believe in paranormal energy of some kind. "No, it's the murders. Don't they tell a lot of gory murder stories on ghost tours?"

Ted dropped the envelope onto the pile. "I'm not really sure. I think that's the French Quarter. I think they talk more about architecture and history on the Garden District tours. It's a different crowd."

"No Hand Grenades?" I laughed picturing the Bourbon Street staple-cocktail – a lime green plastic bottle shaped like a hand grenade with a long bong-like neck filled with some sugary liquor drink and a long, red straw. Some tourists in the Quarter wore a full-size plastic goldfish bowl slung around their neck by a strap with a long straw leading directly from the Kool-Aid-looking drink to their mouths. It was strange that tourists took that for local when they only ever saw each other carrying those hyper-sized cloying concoctions. It was the same with Carnival. Many people came to Mardi Gras for the booze and boobs. Standing among other tourists who'd seen the same movies they'd seen, I suppose they got what they came for. But, the local version of the celebration was babies, barbecues, booze and lots of socializing, dancing and cheering on parading bands and dancers.

Ted glanced up from his next invoice. "I've seen people carry Hand Grenades in the cemetery sometimes."

I slapped my thigh. "Me too, now that I think of it. Yeah, that's weird. They buy it on Bourbon and drag it all the way Uptown for a midday walk in a cemetery? Although, let's face it. If they opened a Tropical Isle across from the cemetery, the place would be littered with those grenade cups."

Ted shook his head and wrote an address on the next envelope. "You're probably right. What time is your tour?"

My spine snapped to full height. "I gotta go."

Our guide was a youngish man with too much beard for his face. That seemed to be all the rage lately despite our climate. He stood at the edge of the sidewalk. "Gather round. Don't be shy. Get to know your neighbor. That's it. Closer. Okay, I'm Max and we have lucked into another hot-as-heck New Orleans summer day."

I was the only one who'd brought an umbrella. Portable shade could make all the difference on a sunny day here.

Max pointed at his ears. "Are you listening? Can you hear me?"

We all said yes.

"I'm gonna give you some NOLA wisdom. When a tour guide tells you to do something – do it!"

I couldn't help but be suspicious of his use of the acronym NOLA. Though it was as legit as SCUBA, the term wasn't usually used by locals.

Max clapped once, snapping us to attention. "I say 'drink water' and you..." He pointed at us.

Most of our dozen-large group answered, "Drink water."

He clapped once, again. "Excellent. We're gonna get along just fine. Okay, so the Garden District was built when the Americans came to New Orleans after the Louisiana Purchase of 1803. The Creoles living in the city named the Garden District for its outsized front gardens. In the context of the time, the name

26

was meant as a derogatory term for the tackiness of putting a garden in the front of the house in a large yard, something they viewed as back-of-the-house. In particular, they found the use of manure fertilizer in a front yard to be gauche. The locals were apparently equally offended by the vulgar grandeur of the large homes, mostly built between 1848 and 1873."

My family had been part of the colonization of our nation so it felt strange thinking of them as the tacky Americans moving to the elegant and cultured city. It was they same way I looked at those tourists with the grenade drinks, the way Patrick and I looked at the wave of hipsters that had recently descended on our city, many from New York and L.A.

We started in Lafayette Cemetery #1, a path I often took while walking the neighborhood. Max explained the local tradition of burying bodies above ground. "One of the most common misconceptions about our city is that we bury people above ground why?" He elongated the "why" as a prompt.

The crowd offered guesses like, "it's under sea level" and "the bodies would pop up."

Max bowed a little then popped back up dramatically. "The water table, right? Popping up like *Poltergeist*, right? Something like that?"

Most nodded. I caught one woman looking at my parasol with envy. I wasn't sure if it was because of the shelter it offered or because it was adorable and edged with ruffles. Lately, I'd started buying fanciful things I'd previously denied myself. During Patrick's Pussyfooter shopping spree, he talked me into letting him give me the most over-the-top necklace in the whole store. The sparkly pink plastic roses looked like iced cupcake toppers. It was the kind of whimsical Barbie-worthy necklace I would've quietly obsessed over when I was five. Or twelve. Or in my forties, but more secretly. It was only twenty dollars and yet I hemmed and hawed over whether it was worth the money. It seemed supremely impractical. Patrick settled it for me and it was downright cathartic. I spent the rest of that day glancing over at the necklace in its clear plastic bag, taking it out to watch it sparkle and staring at it sitting on the coffee table while a smile spread across my face. By midnight I had to admit that I'd already gotten more than twenty dollars worth of joy from the necklace and I hadn't even worn it yet. I felt like a giddy girl at Christmas who'd gotten the exact pretty-princess thing she wanted. It was a big step in my journey away from being driven by practical concerns and toward matters of the heart. Strong, not tough.

Max pointed at a mausoleum that was missing its tombstone. Everyone leaned forward to see the two empty stone shelves. "The casket would be loaded into the top and left sealed up for at least a year and one day. Temperatures six feet under can be as cool as fifty degrees but above ground, this enclosure can reach up to 150 degrees."

The guy in the jean shorts laughed. "It's a crock pot."

The guy in the mismatched Hawaiian shirt and swim trunks corrected, "Pizza oven," then shoved the other guy playfully.

Max shook it off. "If you'll look behind you, I want you to notice a tomb holding thirty-seven people from one family."

The woman who'd envied my umbrella looked disgusted. "In there? Together?"

Max grinned. "It's a far more planet-friendly way to handle our dead. It's basically solar-powered cremation." He swept his arm like a less-feminine Vanna White. "Now, you may recognize this cemetery from the many movies and TV shows it's starred in like *Double Jeopardy*."

Max's tour was mercifully light on gore and heavy on history and context. We wound our way to a former inn where guests and employees reported footsteps, objects moving on their own, lights, appliances and water faucets turning on and off and glimpses of a translucent man. We stopped at one of Ann Rice's former homes for some stories and slowed again in front of a home obscured by gargantuan palm fronds, banana leaves and umbrella plants. It was like its own ecosystem, a patch of rain forest among the topiary, manicured lawns and assortment of Garden District blooms. I had to admit the house looked spooky with its vine-laced columns and towering, heavily curtained windows.

Max waited for us to gather and quiet again. "The House of the Lonely Boy. Built in 1871, the home is said to be cursed and indeed there are some notable deaths. The couple who built the home died within a week of each other leaving their only son to languish alone. He eventually took a wife and they went on to have three children. One of those children died in childbirth. Another died at the age of seven. Only one child remained – a son. Once again, the house claimed its victims. The parents died in the home together when their fireplace became obstructed while they slept and filled the room with smoke before they could save themselves. Some say you can still smell the smoke in the master bedroom on humid days. Like today. This continued on for generations until the current homeowners. Or should I say – homeowner. The current homeowner lost his parents in the late 1970's. As with all the previous family members, they were prominent citizens. Newspapers recount an electrical accident killed the judge, and his fading beauty queen wife passed within a month when she slipped in the master bath and hit her head on the cast iron tub. Local accounts credit The Curse of the Lonely Boy. Only the story's end appears to be in sight as the current owner remains childless and unmarried. He was the family's only son."

Mismatched Hawaiian guy piped up. "How old is he?"

Max looked dramatically toward the jungle-entangled house. "He's no spring chicken." He turned back to us. "Some say the curse has finally caught up with the family. Some say the owner's trying to break the curse by having no children. What we do know is that he was so young when his parents passed that he was raised by his spinster aunt. Some say she was the reason he never married. A superstitious woman, she is said to have chased away any real prospects claiming it was the Christian thing to do. That allowing any woman to live in this house was like ushering them to the guillotine."

Jean shorts guy ribbed mismatched Hawaiian guy again. "It's not paranoia if they're really after you." They were probably drunk.

We stopped at three more homes before landing

in front of my own. I got a pen out just in case. Max told us when it was built and that the family had owned a shop on St. Charles at the turn of the century. Then he started to recount the tale of our family moving here from Texas with their horse, Tex, pulling their possessions across the terrain. "Miss Lily was the daughter of a wealthy plantation owner. Her husband, Leonard Oliver Perry is said to have had a gift for woodwork and opened a shop on St. Charles that remained a lucrative business until the 1930's. Like many Americans at that time, the couple was fleeing their past after the Civil War ended. Though I can't say what they were fleeing, I can say they brought a chandelier with them. The chandelier is said to have belonged to the family's mammy who braved the wagon journey with them."

It felt strange hearing some version of my family story from a stranger. On a tour. In front of other strangers. How many times had this story been told? How many people had heard it?

Umbrella-envy woman raised her hand tepidly. "How did a slave get a chandelier?"

Max smiled. "Yes. She was not a slave anymore. She was a free woman when she traveled with the family."

Jean shorts guy couldn't resist. "If I was freed, I'd run as far from them people as my legs would carry me."

Max decided not to off-ramp into a discussion of why many freed slaves continued to work with the families that had owned them. "I want you to notice the giant magnolia tree in the back of the property behind the house. Underneath that tree lie the bones of Tex. Yes, they buried their faithful horse in the yard. A marker thanks Tex for his faithfulness. If you'll direct your attention to the bedroom window on the upper left, you might be able to catch a glimpse of the chandelier."

Jean shorts guy seemed dissatisfied as he made a visor of his hand. "There's too much glare."

"The chandelier is said to be haunted by the spirit of that mammy. She is said to protect a family secret."

Finally. I blurted, "Which family?"

Max looked my way. "Which family?"

"Yeah, the family that owned the house or the family that owned the chandelier?"

Max's face looked like a frozen computer screen. He seemed genuinely baffled. "The mammy's family I guess."

I tried not to sigh. Had he really not wondered before? "But you don't know." It was more of a statement than a question.

He shook his head. "No, I don't guess I do."

"And you don't know the family secret." Another statement.

Max seemed to suddenly break character. "What I do know is this. If you stand in front of that window long enough, you will see that chandelier move."

My blood rushed. "You've seen it move?"

He snapped back into his routine. "I've witnessed the chandelier swing like a pendulum and once I thought it looked normal from here and then I got closer and realized all of the crystals were sticking straight out like a porcupine."

I remembered that day. Or maybe things

happened when I wasn't home. In either case, I now understood that tourists stood across the street from our house looking at our bedroom window to see the chandelier do its thing. Maybe it was time to close the shutters. Though I would miss waking up to rainbows the morning sun shot through the crystals onto the walls, it would help keep the room cooler for summer.

I'd hoped the tour story would reveal something. I looked down at my notes scrawled on a small pad. 1890's. Texas. Shop on St. Charles. Lily. Leonard Oliver Perry. Wait. Leonard Oliver Perry. Leonard Perry. Leonard Perry? Wasn't that the name on the bill of sale from the Wells Plantation? The overseer my great-great-grandmother ran away with, my great-great-grandfather, was the one who'd come to New Orleans to sell a slave. I'd held a document he signed. A bill of sale for Lottie.

What if it was the same Lottie that was Sassy's great-grandmother? That would mean my great-great-grandfather sold Sassy's great-grandmother, the twins' great-great-grandmother. No matter how common the names Leonard and Lottie may have been at the time, it was becoming less than coincidental that they kept appearing attached to the Wells Plantation. It had to be the same woman. It was beyond ugly but I was so grateful Sassy's family had raised generations of mine. Was that selfish? Certainly privileged. I'd have to tell Taffy and Chiffon.

I stayed after and waited for Max's attention. "Hey, great tour. Thanks. Can I ask you something?"

He chuckled. "Only if I can. Why do people say 'seven sisters' when you walk away?"

33

I was shocked. "It's a movie."

"Any good?"

"I haven't seen it yet. It's not out. They must've seen the trailers or articles or something."

His face grew wide. "You're in it? Cool! I've been thinking about getting into acting here. Seems like there's a lot of work. I studied in college. Kinda why I became a tour guide. I wanted to teach but I don't really like school. I had this idea that I'd wear these costumes and teach without the worries of a classroom and administration and testing and all that. I thought it'd be like acting with breaking the fourth wall, you know?"

I did. "Sure."

"But all they wanna do is drink. That's why I left the Quarter. It's better over here. I thought I'd show off my talent and storytelling. For this I studied Shakespeare, you know?"

I did. "That's showbiz. It's the gap between the way things look and the way things are. What I wanted to know is where y'all got the story for the house with the horse in the back."

"The haunted chandelier house? When you start out as a guide, they give you a list of sites and a script. You do it until you feel comfortable with it but after a while, you find you've added a lot of your own information, your own jokes, details--"

I interrupted, "Embellishments."

Max smiled somewhere in all that beard. "Showbiz. We work for tips too."

"Of course." I dug into my skirt pocket.

"No, I didn't mean…"

I handed him a five.

"Thanks." He pocketed the bill. "I've been doing this a while now so a lot of my stories have been personalized even if they're from the original script but I added this house myself. I'm the only one who does this story."

I felt myself getting closer to some truth. "Where did you get it"

"It's an old story. Everyone from the neighborhood knows it."

I was immediately confused. "Your family's from here? This neighborhood?" Max hadn't struck me as local.

"No, but I know a guy. Guides sometimes share stories."

"He's a guide? Why doesn't he tell the chandelier story?"

"Non-believer. Besides, he works the Quarter."

"Where'd he get the story?"

"It's a neighborhood story and a lot of these families moved here around the same time, been friends and neighbors for generations."

I thought about that. I tried to imagine knowing your neighbors so well, you knew their family stories. I'd moved ten times in my eighteen years in L.A. I rarely knew my neighbors and most weren't friendly when our paths crossed. I tried to imagine growing up here, going to school with the children's children of my family's neighbors. My family had history with some of the people living in these stately homes. The neighbors must've thought the loyal horse to be noteworthy to have passed that story forward, or maybe someone read the tombstone and filled the rest in with gossip. But Max's version was mostly true. "So the ghost story was passed down?"

"The chandelier? I saw that with my own eyes. You will too if you stand in front of that house long enough. Trust me on that."

I was definitely closing the shutters when I got home. I didn't even care if that meant he'd figure out it was my window. "The protector of a family secret."

"Yeah, that was a local legend. For sure. I'm not the only one that's seen the chandelier do its thing. People tend to make their own theories in the wake of seeing something you can't explain. Supposedly there was a secret. They were definitely leaving something behind when they came here. Lots of people in this neighborhood came by their money dishonestly. Coulda been that. Coulda been they stole that chandelier. Who knows? Those can be the best kind of ghost stories. The ones that keep you wondering forever."

I smiled. "Sure. Of course."

"Sometimes when I find I've got extra time, I add another detail to the story. Supposedly, The Protector is passed down as a title. There's a living protector and one on the other side at all times. When the living protector passes, she becomes the protector on the other side of the veil. I say 'she' because it went from mother to daughter. Then the daughter would become the next living protector. Except I think they must've all passed because the chandelier was gone for decades then reappeared a couple years ago."

I felt a little like I was lying by not telling him I'd hung it, but he was way too interested. He'd probably want to come inside and see it. For hours. "Wow."

"Yeah."

I extended my hand. "Thanks. I had a great time and I learned a lot. You're a good teacher."

He blushed under his beard. "Thanks. Good night."

I was still working on my lines when Patrick got home from yoga. I jumped up and greeted him in the hall. "Hey handsome. How was your day?"

"We still have to do your audition?"

I could tell he was tired just thinking about it. He'd clearly had a long day. But I knew he'd rally. Now that I knew what it was like to have a truly supportive partner helping carry my load, it amazed me how I'd survived and accomplished so much of my career alone. And now that more and more of our auditions were being self-taped and emailed in, I would've had to hire someone for every self-taping and travel to their home or studio. There would've been scheduling issues that couldn't be solved by hoping someone would rally for you at nine pm. And it would've been so expensive over time.

I was one of those actors who was "good in a room" so I was sad to miss out on the opportunity to banter. I took direction well so I missed having a casting director's guidance. But it was amazing to be able to audition for projects filming in Atlanta, Texas, Mississippi, Alabama and even L.A. – all from the comfort of my bedroom.

Patrick gave me a kiss, dropped his gym bag on the ground and stood behind the camera I'd set up. "It still looks orange or yellow or something. And a little speckled." He looked over his shoulder then back at the viewfinder. "Shadows from a few of the chandelier crystals."

I repositioned the clamp-lamp affixed to a shelf full of folded shorts and t-shirts and stood on my mark. "Better?"

"It's okay. Here."

He flipped the viewfinder over so it faced me. I could see a couple of shadows lingering. And it was yellowish. "I can fix the color in my computer but we'll just have to live with the rest. That's as good as it's gonna get with it dark out. Thanks baby."

He rubbed his eyes then picked up his script. My hero.

Chapter 4

I didn't want to readjust Sabine's corset too much. She, Christine and Caroline had told me that I might experience a thrill the first time I put on my corset so I'll admit I was a bit bummed that I didn't have my own corset yet for the potential "thrill" moment. As I zipped up the borrowed corset, I even wondered if I would feel nothing. I untwisted my hot pink tank straps and tugged my pink chin-length wig to check it's security. Walking over to the standing full-length mirror, I played with the feathered hot pink fascinator (with rosettes to match my necklace) that Patrick had gotten me during our spree.

Clipping the dramatic topper tilted to one side, I stood back from the mirror. Pink power pulsed through me and I did indeed feel the rush of being a Pussyfooter. In Sabine's wig and corset, I realized I probably looked like her. It hit me that having that thrill moment in someone else's corset forever bonded us in a memory, building the sisterhood that was at the heart of the organization. I tried not to worry that the women would shut me out or be mean to me. I'd wait for an actual problem to arise.

Over the years of acting and modeling, I'd grown accustomed to costuming. I almost never dressed for Halloween anymore. It felt redundant. Ashley the Traffic Tranny told me she never costumed for Fat

Tuesday for the same reason. She didn't even wear her drag. As I took in my hot pink fishnets and white combat boots, I understood drag in a new way. I could create a character that was more myself than I was – super me. Me unleashed. I would have to think about what that meant to me, what it would look like. Whatever it was definitely included this necklace!

I felt a little silly walking to the bus stop alone but Christine Miller would be joining me at the next stop. Would two of us look less ridiculous? I was in such a good mood that I almost didn't notice the bus pulling away from the corner half a block past me. My phone chirped and I froze, pulling it from the hot pink crocheted pocket tied to my waist. Christine texting she'd meet me on the bus. I hit redial and ran like the wind praying she'd pick up.

Christine was full of cheer. "Hey! You're on the bus?"

I felt like a failure. I breathed heavily. "I'm running. I missed it. I'm running."

Her voice ramped up. "It's coming! I see it but I don't see you. Run! I'm hanging up now. Run!"

I could see the bus pulling over about two and a half blocks away. It seemed impossible I'd make it but I had to try. Maybe it was because of my job or maybe it was just "normal" but I sometimes found myself observing my life while I was living it. I caught glimpses of myself in the shop and restaurant windows. It was like watching those old movies they had to turn by hand. My body ran like my powder pink mini skirt was on fire. But my imagination split off and I started to see myself through the eyes of the people sitting in those restaurants and milling racks in shops. I was an absurd pink blur, nearly six feet of mostly leg galloping down the street in heavy-as-heck white Doc Martens. I'd be gone before they could even take it all in for clues as to what it was about.

I was still a block away, having already run three, when I saw the lights on the back of the bus change. No!

As I drew closer, I saw Christine leaning out of the front door waving me on. Through the back window of the bus, people stared at me. One had his phone up recording the scene. Feeling emboldened, I kept at full speed for that last half block, thrilled I'd actually made it. It hadn't hit me yet that I still had my first parade ahead of me. I was just filled with ecstasy – the joy of having made it before the bus pulled off, the thrill of finding I still had a sprint left in my aging bones. It was all over my face as I hugged Christine and thanked the bus driver who smiled, closed the door, and shook her head as she glanced at the side mirror to pull out.

Looking for a seat, I realized everyone was staring at me. A few clapped or smiled as I passed. Others looked unamused.

Christine sat next to the window and I filled in next to her. She laughed. "That was crazy. The driver said I had until the light turned green then she was closing the door no matter what. It felt like the light was red forever. I honestly thought there was no way you were going to make it. It was like the eight days of oil how long that red light was. We got so lucky. You've got an angel."

I smiled. "Yeah, you. Thank you so much for that.

I can't believe I missed the bus. What's the point of the two hours of figuring out how to put all of this stuff on, in what order and whatever? What's the point if you miss the dang bus?"

"But you didn't." The college kid in front of us turned around and showed us a photo on his phone. I was at least as determined and gangly as I'd imagined but I was also hilarious and beautiful in my abandon and whimsy. It was a photo of the kind of moment we'd all had at some point, when you see something that is best described as "Only in New Orleans." I was an #onlyinNOLA moment for someone. I was part of the local color that helped define this place. And I was headed to dance in a parade.

We hopped off at Canal and weaved through the Quarter to where the parade was gathering in front of the Hotel Monteleone. I'd made a living performing for over twenty years and was usually cool as a cucumber, but I suddenly felt nervous. I was used to preparing for a performance, but dance practices hadn't even started. I was used to the insulation of performing in front of dozens of people distracted by their own jobs and a camera or two. The closer we got to the hotel, the thicker the crowds got lining up on the route. And they all had their cameras and phones out.

Gatherings of dance krewes, walking krewes and bands crowded Royal Street. We walked up to a group of women wearing our official uniform and I felt like when I used to be the new girl in school knowing my clothes weren't the "right" labels. I loved my adorable borrowed bob, but their wigs were works of art ornamented with showgirl-worthy feather arrays or decorated top hats. Standing there in my makeshift uniform with first day jitters, Christine walked off with two other pink, laughing women and I wondered if this had been a terrible idea. Almost immediately, the group of women interrupted their own conversations to ask if I was new and introduce themselves. Their names floated in and out of my ears and I was pretty sure I wouldn't recognize most of them at the grocery, but they made me feel very welcome. And everyone loved my sparkly pink rose necklace as much as I did.

As everyone visited, drank and tweaked costumes and routines for over an hour, I realized that this was probably one of the things that was fun. Everywhere I looked were people who loved the city and its traditions enough to dedicate time and money to be a part of it. And now I was one of them.

I wandered a little among the intertwining clusters and took photos for my blog, but I wasn't quite sure how it was going to work for me to blog about being in an event rather than attending one.

Daryl "Dancing Man 504" was there wearing his signature sash and was delighted to find we'd now be parading together. I felt another rush realizing I wasn't just going to know people in this parade, I was a part of it. Someone in the crowd would show photos of us to their friends at home as visual aids to their you-had-to-be-there stories of our culture. Maybe they'd blog about it.

When I got back to our pink clump in the crowd, Caroline was talking to Christine and two guys. I immediately recognized Caroline's towering feathered-mohawk headpiece from past Mardi Gras parades. I was pretty sure I had a few photos of her on my blog. Maybe she could come with me to May Baily's after the parade and check out the flask.

Though I'd never seen *The Dukes of Hazard*, I also immediately recognized John Schneider from childhood lunch boxes and thermoses. He'd always been a cute blonde with a welcoming smile and twinkling blue eyes, but the years had chiseled him into some kind of Marlboro-Man-billboard cowboy or a wizened surfer-dude like Swayze in *Point Break*.

Christine gestured to the other guy. "This is Charlotte that I was telling you about. I hope you don't mind, Charlotte, but I thought it was magnificent."

Everyone started laughing. John put his hand out for me to shake. "We hear you're quite the track star."

I smiled. "Not bad for an old broad in combat boots that haven't been broken in yet."

John laughed. "They are now."

I laughed too. "I hate to talk shop but didn't you do a day or two on *7 Sisters*?"

"Yeah, why? Have you seen it?"

"Not yet. I'm one of the sisters. Charlie."

His face shifted. Was that recognition? "I've seen some of your scenes when Clarence had that motivational screening before we all had to do press."

I was still learning about things I wasn't a part of despite having a good role in this huge movie. John only worked a day or two. He probably wasn't even sure he'd made the cut, but he was getting press because he'd been on TV since 1978. And that was probably fair. There was no point in kidding myself that my name would help sell tickets. And I was far too seasoned to be an exciting newcomer.

John took my hand in his and looked into my eyes. "You were amazing. People are going to remember you." He let my hand go and smiled.

I smiled back. "Wow. Thank you."

Christine smiled too. "You guys were in something together and you're just now meeting?"

The other guy glanced at his watch then pulled John aside to discuss the time.

John turned to the group and waved once. "It was great meeting you. Have a fun time out there."

Caroline waved as he and the other guy walked away. "Wave to us on the route!"

John yelled back over the crowd and speakers mounted on truck-beds pumping dance music. "You got it!"

Christine tried to slap her thigh but landed in layers of ruffles. "Darn it. I meant to introduce you to Robert."

What? "Row bear?"

Christine chuckled. "The French pronunciation of Robert."

I laughed at my rookie mistake. "Right, of course. So who's Ro-bear?"

"Oh, he has a tour you'd probably love. It's the one that goes past your place in the French Quarter."

"Ha! That's funny. I just took the tour that goes past our unit in the Garden District. Actually talks about our house."

"Oh, how weird. Did you learn anything?"

Whistles broke out everywhere as groups detangled from each other and lined up. Sabine waved from a row halfway back and I filled in a hole in the lineup beside her. We hugged then formed lines as more whistles blew. Sabine stuck her arms out like an airplane and I did the same. We touched our middle fingertips and held the pose until the dance leaders in the front lowered their arms.

Sabine smiled. "You ready?"

I crinkled my face. "I'm nervous."

"Yeah but don't be. Just have fun. Seriously. That's the job today."

She sounded like Sofia. Everything about this felt right. Except my nerves. I was beginning to understand the abundance of Jello shots I'd been offered and declined.

The day-drinker, informal block party vibe faded as each group fell into line and started to put on their show. I felt self-conscious and wondered if it was harder to have to remember a bunch of dances or to find something to do with my body for the next couple miles. I was glad the parade was short. Probably no more than an hour.

It seemed like there were more cameras than at Cannes. And the crowd was so close they could high-five us. Maybe this wasn't for me after all. I smiled and danced with as much abandon as I could muster. Whenever dancers passed me in parades, I always gravitated to the ones who were having the most fun. I wanted so badly to be the kind of parader I loved the most, but I felt overwhelmed in a way I hadn't experienced in all those years with Oscars winners and industry veterans. I felt like an obvious novice. An untrained outsider. I hadn't grown up second-lining. I didn't have the fancy footwork ingrained in me. I was more the dance-in-one-spot-and-move-your-hips type. And until moving to New Orleans, it wasn't routine for me to dance in the streets for hours.

Then I remembered the D.J. in me, the college student spinning in a nightclub and dancing six hours a night by myself in a booth overlooking the crowd. I spotted Patrick on the sidewalk and jumped out of our loose formation to kiss him then ran back to my spot. Sabine shot me a reassuring smile and then I did what I did in that D.J. booth – I focused on the music. And it mostly worked.

Patrick waited on the curb as the parade dispersed in front of a bar full of the people who'd already finished. It looked like a technicolor Peter Max version of the *Star Wars* cantina in there. I thanked and hugged Sabine and tried to find Christine in the roaming mass of pink. Caroline's headpiece moved in the distance and I trotted toward it, throwing Patrick the one-minute finger over my shoulder.

Christine grabbed my arm as I brushed past. "How was it?"

I chuckled. "As nerve-wracking and wonderful as a first kiss."

Her pink Marilyn Monroe wig tickled my shoulder as we shared a sweaty hug. "You're good to get home?"

I pointed to the corner half a block away. "Patrick's over there. Tell Caroline I said bye. Hope to see her again soon."

A wedding second line passed as we turned onto our street in the French Quarter. This whole uptown-downtown lifestyle was a fantasy come true for both of us. The Gay Pride parade would roll through the Quarter later in the weekend. For locals, it wasn't that special to be in a parade. It was downright common to attend them. Now we had bathrooms in both major parade locations in the city. Life was good.

After Patrick went to sleep, I downloaded my camera and started a new blog post. Caroline's mohawk-headpiece was truly amazing. It was too bad I didn't suggest we head over to see the flask. It was only about six blocks from the end of the parade. Had my great-great-grandfather Leonard brought it with him when he traveled from Cloutierville to New Orleans to sell Sassy's great-grandmother? And left it in a brothel? I'd always romanticized the man Lily gave up Wells Plantation for, the overseer she found more valuable than generations of wealth, her station in society and an easy way of life. Now he seemed no better than the L.A. stars, agents and producers I'd traded in for a chance at happiness.

I typed "Cloutierville history" into Google and clicked a few links. There had been a skirmish near the town in 1861. That had to be frightening. Maybe that was one reason they left.

The town was on the Cane River and I suddenly wished I'd read that book by the same name on Oprah's book club list. The Cane River region was best known for its Creole culture and the many residents who settled there after buying their freedom. Maybe that was why they took the chandelier when they left the plantation. If they knew of others who'd bought their freedom, maybe they gave Mama Eunoe the chandelier so she'd be ensured freedom. It did seem odd that the same guy who kept slaves in line in the fields and sold a woman would also concern himself with ensuring a slave's freedom.

But *Amazing Grace* was written by an overseer. Anything was possible.

Cloutierville was best known for being a home to author Kate Chopin. Another author I hadn't read. Chopin and her husband had moved there from New Orleans in 1879 and established businesses and raised a large family. Though she tried to run the businesses without him, Kate left not long after her husband's death. Apparently, the home/museum had been destroyed by fire in 2008. One less attraction in Cloutierville.

I had to admit I was looking for an excuse to go up there and look around. There was a giant pecan farm and a cemetery that didn't even begin to rival our local ones in beauty. I clicked through images looking for I-wasn't-sure-what. Something familiar? The land was flat there as were most of the houses. Lots of sprawling ranch homes. Some stores with rusted tin roofs and a house converted to a pecan shop lined the local roads.

There were cotton fields, which creeped me out a little, and live oaks covered in lush growth. Live oaks lived in concert with some type of fern-moss that covered the bark all the way out to the leaves. When it hadn't rained, the fern-fronded moss would shrivel and eventually brown. These photos had clearly been taken after a rain – the branches were thick with lush greenery. The Cane River was unkept in old photos, trees felled along the banks were left to nest birds and snakes.

Less than an hour further north in Natchitoches were parks, plantations and other historical sites and cultural learning centers, but most were about the

Creole history and culture in the area. Definitely a place worth exploring, but not really a reason to drive to a town south of there with a pecan shop and a burned-down museum.

I closed all the windows except the blog entry and focused. As usual, I started by reliving the day through photos. Wide smiles on my new friends, shots of dance krewes and stilt walkers visiting while sipping go-cups. Dancing Man 504 posing with me in my borrowed corset and wig. I'd lived an amazing life in L.A. walking red carpets in glamorous gowns, dating big wigs and working on amazing projects with some of the best in our business. But I'd never looked as happy in any of those photos as I did in my Barbie-toned confections with my arm around Daryl's sweaty shoulder.

Chapter 5

Uncle Lionel was a you-had-to-be-there type of experience as a person and a performer. And he had passed on. A real lady killer, he was always dressed in a suit and hat when he wasn't in his black and white Treme Brass Band uniform. Like any local character, he had mythology. My favorite story was that his mother had been one of the ladies of the night in Storyville who'd started the Baby Dolls, the Mardi Gras crashers that inspired the Pussyfooters a century later.

Uncle Lionel wore his wristwatch strapped across his hand because he always said he had "time on his hands." I loved running into him on the street and almost always reminded him that he still had the sexy. I chose him as my Favorite Local Character 2011 for my blog.

At a backyard party in 2010, Uncle Lionel redefined the drum solo for me. Built like a senior Don Knotts and armed with mallets, a big bass drum and grinding hips, Uncle Lionel's solo was characterized by groove. Well placed thuds punctuated slow rhythmic gyrations. He basically turned the big sphere into a lover – no, a phallus. It was fun, cool and dang sexy.

At a Trombone Shorty concert, the band was gearing up for one of Trombone Shorty's showiest moments where he holds a note on his trumpet without stopping for over three minutes. Uncle Lionel joined the stage and put the amazing Troy "Trombone Shorty" Andrews in momentary check. He held his umbrella over his shoulder and played it like a trombone as he "sang" an imitation of the instrument. It was amazing. Eighty years old, he got his sexy on and played a hell of an umbrella to the delight of the crowd. Trombone Shorty's note was amazing but he knew he'd been bested by a geriatric playing an umbrella.

Performing since he was eleven years old, Uncle Lionel was an institution. But the cool kind – like Snoop Dogg as a senior citizen banging on a bass drum topped with a cymbal. Uncle Lionel made his own drum, then used it to stay afloat during The Storm. In 2010, that drum was stolen and local radio station, WWOZ, put out the word. *Gambit Weekly* featured a story shaming the culprit, "You do not steal a man's drum. Especially if he's still alive and beating it." The drum was returned within a day.

Eighty-one and ailing, Lionel Batiste had seen his end coming and wanted to attend his own second line. I was sad he wouldn't be with us. Uncle Lionel's drumbeat was the pulse of this city. Local musicians would parade every night until his funeral.

When Christine's tour guide friend, Robert, shared the sad news with the group, I was the only one who gasped. Robert tried to contextualize the city's loss but I could see the tourists weren't able to imagine Uncle Lionel's talents, quirks and natty style condensed into a Prince-sized powerhouse.

As we entered St. Louis Cemetery #1, Robert

paused outside the gate to let everyone catch up.

A woman in a yellow visor yelled out, "Is this the best cemetery?"

Robert's expression was serene but I could see he didn't love the question. "This is my personal favorite. Lafayette #1 is beautiful and I love the trees. Lafayette #2 has great iron work, but I love cemeteries because that's where history is buried. It's where we can pay respect to what they created. For that, this is the best cemetery."

That seemed to satisfy the woman.

Robert gestured toward the gate of the oldest cemetery in the city and launched into its history. As a fan of *Easy Rider*, I knew the place immediately. Without permits or permission, Dennis Hopper and Peter Fonda, playing counter-culture bikers, brought Toni Basil and Karen Black, playing prostitutes, to film a long segment in the cemetery where their characters dropped acid. Maybe it was wrong or sacrilegious, but I'd always liked that scene, even the image of Fonda tripping in the statue-arms of the monumental Italian Benevolent Society Tomb. Apparently the architect, Pietro Gualdi, hated our city, but died of malaria and was one of the first to be buried within the tomb.

Of the thousands of bones laid to rest in the city block, several belonged to notable figures. St. Louis Cemetery #1 was the Forest Lawn of New Orleans. Homer Plessy, the 1892 version of Rosa Parks, shared the resting place with Bernard de Marigny (after which the Faubourg Marigny section of New Orleans was named), who brought the game of Craps to the United States. Gamesman Paul Morphy was one of the first world champions of chess. Benjamin Henry Boneval Latrobe was credited with bringing the profession of architecture to the United States and designed the United States Capitol and the Baltimore Basilica, the first Roman Catholic Cathedral in the U.S.

The tomb for those who'd fought in the Battle of New Orleans, the greatest and final land victory of the war of 1812 against the British, was fairly disappointing. Though I wasn't much for war stories, I loved the tale of the rich, poor, old, young, male, female, Catholic, non-Catholic, pirate and politician of every heritage all coming together to defend our city and the entire Louisiana Purchase. Never mind that the war had already officially ended without word reaching the south.

But, perhaps the most well known resident of the cemetery was Voodoo priestess Marie Laveau, the local-born free woman of mixed descent who died at ninety-nine years old in 1881. Like Jim Morrison's grave in France, the tomb had become a destination for many and was defaced daily. Apparently, someone a few decades ago spread the rumor that inscribing three X's on Miss Marie's tomb would get your wish granted. Both the defacing and the constant cleaning degraded the tomb.

Whether it was coming from within or from the adulation of the living, the power of the graffitied tomb was palpable. Many people had left offerings from candy to coins. There was even a gossip magazine, a koozie and a yo-yo. As we waited, a young man came to practice his religious rituals and make his offerings. Like Catholics, Voodoo practitioners believed that there were spirit go-betweens who could help us confer with our God. Catholics called these go-betweens saints. Voodoo called them ancestors. I liked that idea. As with Catholicism, in Voodoo it was believed that we needed priests to help us curry favor with these go-betweens, to petition the dead for help. Though Marie Laveau's mystical powers may have derived more from her time spent as a hair dresser to the rich (and an ear for their secrets) than from the ancestors, she remained perhaps the most famous Voodoo priestess.

Robert drove home the idea that our dead were with us. "We carry their names, their history and many of their beliefs." He talked about how some people kept their loved ones alive by interacting with their dead. This idea was especially evident with the tomb painted swimming-pool blue and decked with silk flowers. Apparently, the doting son of the woman laid to rest there changed the tomb regularly to please his mother. The latest incarnation was a tribute to her favorite color.

I thought about the ancestors I carried with me. We'd had many deaths in my family and my youth was peppered with funerals for friends, relatives and even my college roommate. I carried those souls with me like a bouquet of helium balloons – something light and barely tethered to the Earth, but sometimes bulky and hard to fit through doors. I liked the Egyptian idea that speaking the names kept people alive, made them immortal. I wasn't the type to bring flowers to a grave. I didn't even know where most of my dead were buried. My memory was my graveyard. After surviving a couple dozen deaths, I'd created my own Memorial Day where I went through the names, the memories, the losses. It was like roll call for my "pearly gates" reception party, but it also helped me give shape to my grief. Setting aside one day helped keep me from dwelling in the past when I was endeavoring to live in the present. And I could take stock of my pain – feel which wounds were healing, which had left hardened scar tissue and which wounds hadn't even been addressed.

Robert led us out of the cemetery and through Armstrong Park into the Quarter. The tour passed my front door without stopping. I noticed yellow visor woman trying to see through our shutters. Our neighbor was standing on his stoop with his dog. He jiggled a key in the lock and spotted me walking toward him. He smiled, then looked puzzled as he realized I was with the tour group. I shrugged and he laughed as the door pushed open.

Behind the next stoop, a drunken tourist peed on the beautiful yellow camelback house with robin's egg blue trim. I hated that. People peed on our house all the time. It made no sense to me. Would they be okay with me peeing on their houses? And there was never a time when you couldn't find a bathroom in the French Quarter if you were willing to buy a drink or something. And if you weren't willing to pay for drinks, meals, music or souvenirs – why would you come to the city? It made no sense. Unless it was a simple lack of respect for our neighborhood.

Yellow visor woman half-covered her face as we passed the wavering drunk. Robert stepped beside her, helping to block her view. "I'm so sorry. There was no call for you to see something like that.

Appears to be over-served."

She laughed uncomfortably. "That's okay. My friends warned me about the local color."

Robert stopped, his face losing it's humor. "No! I'm local color. That's a drunken ass." He took a breath, turned and continued toward Bourbon.

I truly loved that Robert stood up for our culture. He was probably born here. I caught up with him and matched our strides. "Thanks for that. I live on that block."

Yellow visor lady interjected. "You live here?"

I nodded and smiled.

"In the French Quarter?"

"Yes."

She looked genuinely confused. "I don't know what I thought. I guess I never really thought about regular people living here. I guess I just thought the French Quarter was for shopping, eating and drinking."

I smiled at Robert. "Maybe that's why they pee on our houses. They don't know they're houses. Except why are they peeing on any building? No. No excuse for turning someone's home into a toilet."

He chuckled. "Hold firm."

"So, you live here too?"

"In the Quarter? No. Uptown."

I smiled at the beautiful redhead walking home from Trashy Diva as she passed us on the sidewalk. Her hair was done up like a vintage pinup with a curl rolled on either side of her face. She often passed our stoop on her way home from the dress shop where she worked. I loved the daily fashion show. Today's selection was a blue sundress with white polkadots and large white-trimmed pockets. It looked like something Lucille Ball would wear.

I followed Robert as he made the turn back to the coffee shop where we'd started. "I just went on a tour Uptown. A ghost tour. Do you give those?"

He smiled and took me in for a minute. "Not my cup of tea."

"You don't believe in ghosts?"

He seemed to be deciding what to reveal. "I don't believe but I'm fine with stories and enjoying a beer and getting scared by black cats. Not vampires though. Those are ridiculous."

I laughed. "Gotta draw the line somewhere."

"Indeed. Not a fan of that, though." Robert pointed to a for-rent sign that read, "Not haunted." The sign for the unit next door read, "Haunted."

I shook my head. Those've been popping up everywhere lately."

"I find it off-putting. It minimizes death. Loss. Finality."

Exactly. "Yes. That's exactly what it does. But, it's part of what the folks come to see."

He lowered his voice conspiratorially. "Yes, that local color they've heard so much about."

I laughed. "I hope I didn't ask too many questions."

Robert stopped in front of the coffee shop and planted his fists on his hips. "Not at all. You had great questions. This is why I'm a tour guide. I get to talk about how awesome we are, how special this place is, this culture. I love those kinds of questions."

"Oh good." I slipped him a tip and thanked him. "See ya around the neighborhood."

My landline was ringing when I walked in the door of the Garden District place. Sofia. Mark must've still been out of town for me to be getting this much attention. "Hey!"

"Oh good, you're home."

"Just got in. Meant to be. What's up?"

"So? How was it? How was the parade?"

I put Patrick's mail on his short pile and threw out the junk mail before flopping on the love seat. "Honestly, it was harder than I thought in some ways. It was amazing and fun, but it was more nerve-wracking than I thought it'd be. I had like some sorta stage fright or something."

She laughed. "Seriously? Why?"

I flipped through my mail then tossed it on the coffee table. "I'm not used to people paying attention to me that way. It was different having the crowd right there."

"I didn't even think of that. Oh. Yeah, that's different than sitting in a theatre with everyone looking at something you did months ago."

"Yeah, some well-lit, edited, perfected thing. And maybe it's your ninth take."

Sofia laughed. "But wait, aren't there always like a million people running around when you work?"

"Yeah, but they're working. They're not standing two feet from you with their phone in your face. It was just different. I felt self-conscious."

Sofia laughed again. "Which is like the opposite of how to have fun. It's like if I wanted to make a happiness cake and put vinegar in it for no reason."

I laughed too. Sofia always got me going. "I didn't do it on purpose. I'm telling you how it felt.

But I kept going. Sabine said to just smile and shimmy and I did. I tried to just focus on the music and have fun."

"Good!"

"Yeah. It was. I think I'll feel better when I know some of the dances. It'll give me something to focus on and maybe that'll help. And I know I'll feel better when I have my regulation uniform. They're making new corsets this year so we don't get them until right before the Blush Ball. And there's other parades before that so I wish I had it already."

Sofia laughed. "You're so into the costume."

Was I? "I think it's 'cause I already know how much a costume can affect performance. I wanted to feel like a diva or something but I felt a little like the new girl, you know?"

"Being the new girl can be fun. I was the new girl in school when we met. And that was fun, right?"

I had no argument for that. So I laughed. "Right."

"Okay, forget all your stupid in-your-head stuff. How were the other... what are they?"

I hated these moments, the moments when I'd realize that we were living very separate lives and that she couldn't even really imagine mine without visiting. "The Pussyfooters."

"The Pussyfooters. How were the other Pussyfooters? Were they nice?"

"They're all kind of amazing. Oil executives and scientists and teachers and mothers and whatever. And they all introduced themselves and asked if I was new and they all said the exact same thing. 'You're gonna have so much fun.' After like the third one, I started wondering if it was a cult or something.

Like they were all reading from the same script, or they were Stepford Wives men had tricked into dancing around in underwear."

Sofia was laughing so hard she was crying.

"What?" I started chuckling at her cry-laughing.

She tried to speak, but only squeaky nonsense made it's way out. Which only made me laugh harder. She tried again. Something about a sickle? That didn't make sense. Sofia tried again. "So si--" She dissolved into gasping laughter again.

It was getting harder for me to speak through my own laughter. "Sick? Sickle?"

Sofia was lost in laughter. She pulled me in with her and we were teenagers again. When she finally calmed a little, she managed, "So cynical."

I laughed even harder. "Cynical! That makes more sense than sickle." We both laughed some more, then I wound down. "That's terrible. Oh my gosh, I'm so cynical."

Sofia laughed, then calmed, laughed again and calmed again. "Yeah, but you're not like you used to be. You're good. This is good. I'm really glad you're doing this."

""People in L.A. think they're so laid back. They have no idea what that means. It's not supposed to mean not caring. These people have perfected enjoying life. It's like an art form here. Oh, and they were great."

Sofia paused. "What was?"

"The women. The Pussyfooters."

She started laughing again. "I thought you meant some piece of art." The laughing escalated. "And I was like – why are we talking about art?"

I laughed too. "Art Garfunkel? Art Vandelay?"

That was it, the cry-laughing took her over again.
I loved her abandon.

Chapter 6

Aunt Ava was excited for Mom's upcoming visit and wanted to hammer out details. Lillibette was getting the house ready and was stressed over arrangements. It seemed like an awful lot of activity over sisters visiting.

While I had Lillibette on the line I decided to risk annoying her. "Can you remember to get the photo album out from the attic? I can have Mom look when she gets there if your plate is too full."

"I'll remember this time. I have to go up there today anyway."

"Great. I'll bring you some pralines if you want."

Lillibette laughed. "We're having cake when y'all visit but don't let me stop you."

It was another muggy July day for the two mile walk to the post office, but I liked doing most of my errands on foot. I'd been using my car less and less even before the air conditioning died. I liked walking, going slow, taking in quirky details of the mansions and wrought iron fences. Playful decorations personalized everything from doors and fencelines to lampposts and street signs. Nothing escaped this city's love for festooning and bling. I liked being able to smell the sweet olive, jasmine and gardenias and enjoy the cornucopia of blooms in the eponymic gardens. Summers were gorgeous in the Garden

District.

Though there were far more homes on far smaller lots now and cars were parked along the roads, it was easy to imagine being in another time. Horse-headed iron posts still invited you to tie your horse. Carriage houses and the horse drawn carriages offering tourists a trip through time all served as reminders that these potholed streets were once dirt. It was easy to picture women with hoops and boning under their cumbersome clothes accompanied by men in hats. Actually, the men here still wore hats. But it was easy to picture a time before cars, TV's, phones and computers, a time of eating meals together made without microwaves or drive-thrus, a time of speaking to people only in person or by letter, a time of candlelight and piss pots. Though I carried my umbrella for shade, sweat gathered in the elastic of my tank top's shelf bra. It must've been such a burden to wear all those layers in a time before air conditioning and indoor plumbing. I loved being able to rinse off after a long walk and dry in the cool of electrically-enhanced air.

The sidewalks were broken and kicked up by live oak roots instead of earthquakes. Some sidewalks were stone, some slate, some herringbone brick and some regular poured concrete. Most were marked by white ceramic tiles spelling out the street names in azure letters lined in gold.

Another tall redhead walked past me and we nodded and smiled to each other. Tall people noticed other tall people. It was often the same with redheads. I'd always felt like an oddball in the other cities I tried to call home. I'd been called names, pointed out or made exceptional. Here, I was fairly average. And I loved it. At 5'10" I was never the tallest woman in a room. Since I was the shortest in my family, that felt like normal to me. In L.A., I'd felt like I did in high school - destined to stand in the back row with the tall boys. Though redheads made up less than two percent of the world's population, I once counted fourteen natural-redhead Saints fans in our section of the Superdome. And in a town rife with award-winning musicians, chefs and artists, I wasn't especially talented, worldly or accomplished.

Most importantly, my heart was average here. Plenty of people treated everyone with respect and put others first in this place. The lack of interaction and good manners in New York and Los Angeles shocked me. By the time Sofia moved to L.A., I was used to people not holding doors or even acknowledging each other's existence with eye contact. I saw it all clearly again through Sofia's fresh eyes and reactions.

In front of me, a couple in their twenties pointed at something on their phone. I stopped and took my earbud out. "Y'all finding everything okay?"

I pointed at the corner and directed them to the house where *Benjamin Button* was filmed then motioned to the house beside us. "This is actually the oldest house in the neighborhood." As they expressed surprise at the architecture, I realized I'd become that woman I'd always romanticized – the local lady out walking in a flouncy skirt and lipstick carrying a ruffled parasol. Since I could never be a native, I cherished moments when I felt like I was a local.

Patrick had the pedigree. His parents met at LSU

like mine, but he was born in the city. He grew up waving to family, friends and neighbors throwing beads from floats. He'd survived The Storm, had helped rebuild and knew exactly what "the smell" smelled like.

I wasn't part of this city's fabric in that way. The best I could hope for was to be a local, a part of carrying on all that had come before me. But Patrick and other native New Orleanians might always see me as a "New Dat," someone who came when the city and the Saints were at their peak and stayed for the party. It mattered that I'd come for a family funeral and that I was living in my family's home, but I'd never have the right answer to "where'd you go to school?" People didn't even bother to ask. But for this young couple, I was the local lipsticked-lady with a parasol who knew the landmarks.

The line at the post office was long but many of us were grateful for the extra time in air conditioning. My favorite woman was working and we were both happy I cued up to her. She usually wore her salt-streaked hair in puffy twisted braids around her face. She seemed to be fairly simple about her beauty but I couldn't help but wonder if she had some alternate colorfully-costumed personality in a parade krewe or social aid and pleasure club.

Her no-nonsense face warmed with a smile. She opened her drawer and pulled a sheet of stamps out, dramatic photos of Edith Piaf and Miles Davis. "Wasn't sure about these but I know you like the women's history ones. Figured everybody like Miles."

I was still adjusting to strangers treating me like

family. I'd felt it every time I visited growing up. Once I was in a grocery line of three people. By the time I checked out, the woman in front of me had invited me to her family reunion. She waited for me to check out so I could follow her there.

"They're beautiful. Yeah, I wouldn't have thought to ask for anything like this. Thank you." The stamps weren't a bullseye, but I was moved that she'd pulled them aside who knows how long ago and had been waiting for me to come in again so she could make me happy. In L.A., I'd do little thoughtful things like that for people and it almost invariably pushed them away, especially the guys. Many explained they weren't deserving of my thoughtfulness. I never knew what I was supposed to say to that. Eventually I learned to just believe them.

Lots of people asked why I left Los Angeles. I'd just produced a movie with Clarence Pool. The critics hated it but singled my work out as a highlight, so it should have been time to double down on my career. It should have been time to network and parlay, not pull stakes and become a local hire in a secondary market. I'd had to start over in a town where no one knew me, and audition for leftover bit parts after the lead roles had already been cast in L.A. Then Clarence put me in his latest movie as a local hire and things felt like they'd come full-circle somehow, like I was where I was meant to be, doing what I was supposed to be doing.

The rule was that you were always hottest before a project came out. Your part was as big and important as you said it was and none of it was on the cutting room floor yet. The critics hadn't been consulted. Audiences hadn't reacted. Box office grosses hadn't been counted. With no information to the contrary, the movie was a blockbuster with critical acclaim and your role was big and important. After the project came out, it could be *Transgression*, a movie critics hated and audiences didn't see where only one of your scenes survived the cut. So any sane person would've gone to L.A. the minute they wrapped *7 Sisters* and used that heat to hustle up a TV series, or a bigger, better movie role or two. Patrick had said he'd understand if I went back for a while. But I'd never been more certain that I was making the best choice for a full and happy life. I was where I was meant to be, doing what I was supposed to be doing and that was more than enough.

Passing a small cluster of tourists staring at phones, I turned onto Magazine Street. I still looked for Albert when I walked his section. I couldn't have said we were "close," I didn't even know his last name until he was already gone. Though he'd passed shortly after I relocated, the "Moses of Magazine Street" had been the first person to befriend me here. I could still see him sitting in front of the Design Within Reach storefront, his greying dreads dangling long past his shoulders. It was odd seeing the memorial photo of him as a young man. He'd served in the military and his hair was cropped short under a perky cap. Whatever had made his eye milky hadn't happened yet.

Albert was one of those beautiful souls who always had a kind word for passersby and still managed to make each of us feel special. And I'd met Patrick at his funeral so I was indebted to Albert for that last blessing. It was something I wished I could've told him, thanked him for with a big hug. Since Albert was so ingrained in my first memories after moving here, I'd probably always see him on Magazine. That comforted me.

It felt like a small rebirth to rinse the walk's perspiration off of my sticky skin. I wasn't sure what to expect at Reuben's cocktail party. He'd said we'd be meeting potential investors for his movie so I put on a fitted, black dress left over from my party days in L.A. and tried to organize my humidity-pumped curls into a style. My agent Claudia had set up a meeting with Reuben when I was still "just visiting" after Sassy's funeral. He'd been a fan of my work and wanted to offer me a lead in his next movie. The catch was he hadn't financed it yet. But Claudia had vouched for Reuben and we hit it off right away. Now I was a couple of years into waiting for the money to materialize so I was happy to put on a party dress and schmooze if it meant finally getting the movie off the ground.

I took Patrick's hand and guided him through the crowd of cocktail-sipping potential investors mixing with local actors I recognized from audition waiting rooms. This was familiar. The air smelled of hope and hype. I wasn't sure if any of the other actors were already attached to the film, and I'd seen a few producers come and go already so I wasn't entirely sure which of these people might already be my boss or costar. Life as an actor was almost never about comfort zones.

Reuben motioned to us through the crowd. We made our way to his spot at the bar. "Charlotte, I want you to meet Victor and Jernard."

I hugged Reuben then extended my hand to the blue-suited Victor, and Jernard who wore a Drew Brees jersey over black slacks and dress shoes.

"Charlotte's the one I was telling you about."

Victor and Jernard nodded. Then Jernard jolted. "Oh snap. You're the one what worked with Clarence Pool?"

I smiled, feeling that familiar awkwardness associated with selling myself as a product. "Three times actually."

Victor became animated. "Right. You was in *Tickled* like ten years ago." He hit Jernard. "She was the one in the champagne scene." He nodded to Patrick. "This your wife? Respect man."

Patrick smiled. "Not yet."

Jernard laughed. "Better put a ring on it."

Tucked in Patrick's arm, I'd missed his expression but whatever it was made the men smile quietly.

Jernard nodded. "Yeah, you set."

Victor was apparently a pretty big fan of my work and wanted to talk about roles I'd played in the 90's. He knew all four of my lines from *Tickled* – which was equal parts flattering and odd given the movie was ten years old and my part was so small.

Patrick spotted Wendy waving at us and tapped me to get my attention.

I still wasn't sure who Victor and Jernard were so I waved back and waited for the conversation to lull. "Are y'all staying a while? We just got here and I see a friend I need to say hi to."

"Of course." Victor extended his hand. "We're here. Probably won't move five feet from this bar."

Jernard and Reuben laughed. They seemed like old friends. Maybe they grew up together.

Wendy was wearing a leafy-print sundress cinched with a wide green belt. I always liked hugging tall women. It felt comforting and familiar since I was an inch shorter than my mother. Wendy hugged Patrick, careful not to spill her drink as she reached over his shoulders. "You just getting here?"

I scanned the faces in the room. "Pretty much. Got any idea who we're supposed to impress?"

"No. I figured you would. You always know that kind of stuff."

I chuckled. "Must be rusty. But I don't really have my finger on the pulse of this. Lotta people already come and gone without me knowing, much less predicting. I think we've already gone through two husbands for me and three producers that I don't see anywhere around."

Wendy nodded. "I can't tell if it's a bad sign."

"It's not odd. I will say that. By the time we finally shot *Transgression*, that movie I produced with Clarence, only me, Clarence and the writer-director were still there. It's hard to tell the difference between a movie that's difficult to get made and a movie that will never get made. Especially now that you can make a movie on a phone. Claudia says Reuben's tenacious and respected. Now that I know what it can take, those are things worth banking on for me. It took nearly a decade to get *Transgression* made. Anything less than that's probably a win and Reuben was already a couple years in when I met him a couple years ago. I figure we're nearly there if it's gonna happen."

We decided to keep the faith and started schmoozing with the group of straight-from-work-dressed people and two women in head-to-toe black next to us. I hoped Patrick wasn't too miserable. I knew he didn't love meeting lots of strangers at once. The women in black were from New York. They'd just taken the tour through St. Louis Cemetery #1 and past our stoop in the French Quarter.

Wendy laughed. "I used to lead that tour."

I laughed too. "I just took that tour."

Wendy laughed bigger. "You took a tour?"

"Two actually. I took the haunted Garden District one that starts in Lafayette #1 and goes past the Garden District place."

Wendy laughed again. "I used to know the guy who did that one. That tour goes past his house too. Funny, right? I think now he does the one you guys just took. What did your guide look like?"

One of the New Yorkers waved her hand dismissively. "Like he was stuck in the 1800's. Long hair, beard, but not like what's happening now. Shakespearian."

I smiled. "So, no man bun." I wasn't a big fan of the man bun.

"No. Nothing stylish. Just regular clothes and a bunch of hair."

Though I liked his flowing, slightly disheveled hair, I was pretty sure they were describing Robert. "Do you remember his name?"

The New Yorker lady stirred her cocktail. "His name? No. It was something weird I think. Pierre?"

"It sounds like Robert. That's the guy who led our group."

Wendy's eyes went wide. "That's who I was talking about! Robert. He's the one who used to do the haunted Garden District tour and now does the French Quarter one."

I chuckled. "Wow. Small world." A gasp. "Wait, which house was his house? You said his house was on the tour. Do they tell a story about it?"

Wendy swirled her cocktail straw around her glass of mostly ice. "The Lonely Boy house. Do they still tell that one?"

I hoped the New Yorkers weren't investors because we were all but ignoring them now. "Wait. Robert is the lonely boy? The cursed child?"

Wendy shook her head. "He hates that. Don't tell him you know."

"Is any of it true?"

Wendy laughed. "Ghost stories? Curses? Who knows. I've seen things I can't explain. Heck, even Robert's having second thoughts now – and he was the biggest sceptic I knew."

Patrick perked up.

"He saw something?" I was probably fishing for people who'd believe the things I'd seen the chandelier do.

"He got some artifact or something from a graveyard and now his house is acting up. I mean there's a grain of truth to all those stories on that tour. The historical data is mostly right. The dates and names and stuff. The rest is usually open to opinion."

"But his house is suddenly haunted? After he got this object or whatever?"

Patrick jumped in. "What was it?"

Wendy looked up. "He told me but I forget.

Something mailed to the office, I wanna say."

Patrick offered, "So, not an elephant."

Wendy laughed. "That narrows it down."

I was still feeling pretty serious. "What does the house do?"

"There's a smell of perfume. Lights. Sounds. That sort of thing."

Patrick smiled at me. "Lights. You love that."

I nudged him and smiled at Wendy. "Patrick thinks I'm seeing things--"

He stopped me. "I didn't say that."

I took a breath. "Patrick is having trouble believing that I've seen the chandelier do really weird things since the day we hung it. Stuff physics can't explain. But he's never seen it so..."

Wendy nodded as she finished a sip through her straw. "I get it. Until I saw the stuff I've seen – I get it. It's easier to think we were mistaken. Then you don't have to think new thoughts. But I have to keep an open mind now. I don't really have a choice."

I nodded. "Exactly." It felt good having an ally.

We mingled with strangers who passed our group, swung by Victor and Jernard holding down the bar then found Reuben before heading out. The twinkly lights above him reflected on his freshly shaved head. Reuben's skin was so smooth, I couldn't tell if he was closer to my age or Patrick's. The things we had in common were the only reason I guessed him to be around forty or so. But I'd been mistaken before, I thought Patrick was my age and he thought I was his for a few weeks before we discovered the ten years between us. Men in L.A. almost never had grey hair so I had no idea men in their thirties could be salt-

and-pepper. I was still getting used to the idea of a younger man, but only the idea. The man fit me just right.

I really wanted the chandelier to act up before we turned in. I even brought up Sassy, Mama Heck and Mama Eunoe while I was turning down the bed. But nothing happened.

Chapter 7

Friday the thirteenth started with the good news that quarterback Drew Brees finally signed his contract with the Saints. We'd waited months to hear. Brees was more than just a Super Bowl MVP who'd broken so many records, he'd begun lapping himself and breaking his own. He was a man who'd embraced this city when it was on its knees and dragged it back into jubilance. He'd gotten dirty rebuilding, visited the sick and disadvantaged, donated time and money, and met his devoted fans with grace and kindness. He was more than a legendary athlete, he was a symbol of the city's resilience and investment in itself. The idea that we might lose all of that to some team with a bigger paycheck had the city biting nails for so long that it became irritating. We started wondering just how much it was going to take to buy this guy's loyalty for five more years. But as Patrick woke me with the news, all of that evaporated.

Owing to the Bountygate scandal, we wouldn't have a general manager, defensive coordinator or assistant head coach for at least the first six games this season. And for the first time in as long as anyone could remember, the NFL suspended the head coach for the entire season. With Drew Brees' name finally on that contract, we could go back to believing that there was still a chance to be the first team to ever play a Super Bowl on their own turf.

It was raining big, floppy drops as we made our way to Tuba Fats Square in the Treme. The memorial square was dedicated to the preservation of music from the historic Treme neighborhood, the first black suburb in America. People from all over the city gathered to parade in memory of their favorite Uncle. Musicians played in the crowded Candlelight Lounge next door, the home of Uncle Lionel's regular Wednesday gig with the Treme Brass Band.

Second lines usually included umbrellas, but many were more decorative than functional. Despite the downpour, most folks still opted for decorative or nothing at all. Singing and dancing in the rain was par for the course in New Orleans. Even the encroaching thunder and lightning couldn't scare away the growing crowd.

A funeral commemorated someone's death, but a memorial second line celebrated their life and their influence on the community. Uncle Lionel brought a lot of joy to a lot of people. His Facebook fan page listed sentiments from as far away as Norway, Australia, France and Belgium among many other nations, and dozens of cities in the U.S.

A few people carried memorial photos surrounded by ribbon bows and mounted on sticks. I wore my fleur de lis bracelet across my left hand as Uncle Lionel had always worn his watch. I noticed a few people had done the same with their watches. I even saw someone imitating Uncle Lionel's flair when holding a go-cup – as if it had a handle, with his thumb on the lip and his pinky underneath the cup.

Groups comprised of musicians from a variety of beloved local bands formed at the beginning of the line and the end. Many people wore white, as Uncle Lionel had requested. As the front band struck up *I'll Fly Away* and got the line rolling, I became overwhelmed with emotion. There was something so beautiful about everyone coming together to celebrate this local legend. And I was sad that I'd never run into him again, never watch him bang that drum.

My tears blended with rain but, as the tempo picked up, the sun poked out of the clouds. We headed to Rampart, clothes dripping with warm rainwater and sweat. In a city where community was king, one of my favorite things about second lines was the hugging. I ran into over half a dozen friends and acquaintances – and I didn't even grow up here. Ted from the book store was there, Dancing Man 504 splash-danced with us for a while and we even ran into Margie Perez, a wonderful singer I'd met through the only other guy I'd dated here. My birthday week would start with an open house in a few hours, so Patrick and I made sure to invite all of them.

As we meandered down Rampart toward Sweet Lorraine's Jazz Club, we crossed the neutral ground and dance-walked straight into oncoming traffic. The second line was permitted officially and one side of the street had been closed to make way, but parades could grow an energy of their own. That said, we didn't usually wander through traffic. The cars and buses had no choice but to wait for our mob to dance through them. Almost anywhere else, drivers would've honked and rebelled. Here parades often held up traffic, so many drivers bopped along with our music. Some even abandoned their cars in the street and joined the party.

Christine Miller and Caroline Bozier danced on the sidewalk ahead. Both wore fabulous fascinators and I wondered how many feathery confections they'd collected. When I'd returned Sabine's wig, she showed me part of her collection. A long shelf held styrofoam heads wearing mostly pink hairstyles from Marilyn Monroe to Marie Antoinette. An orange wig reminded me of Farrah Fawcett and I loved the white one with snowflakes and a styrofoam candy cane. Sabine said she had a bunch more and pulled out a plastic tub, lifting the lid to reveal at least a dozen more wigs in pink, orange, green and even rainbow. It was a pretty dazzling display. I suddenly longed for more storage space.

Even with two places to live, we had only two closets total – a small coat closet and a narrow converted hallway where a staircase used to be before cousin May renovated the Garden District place. When most homes in New Orleans were built, closets were taxed as rooms so people used furniture instead - wardrobes, drawers, trunks and bed chests. My last place in L.A. had seven closets, including a walk-in so large it had two different entrances. All of those closets were full.

In L.A., I considered it practical to stockpile premiere dresses or fabulous shoes for last minute invites. I still had two gowns I hadn't worn when I moved here, which came in handy. But I no longer bought gowns for no reason. And I had more than enough impractical heels for a city with sidewalks designed to eat shoes and trip people. Now I had three puffy petticoats instead. A green one (with matching wig) for St. Patrick's, a fuchsia one for the Muses parade and a pink one because a friend from L.A. sent it for my birthday. I planned to wear that one tonight.

Christine spotted me first. "Hey!"

I waved and shouted over the music as I danced through the crowd toward them. "Hey! Y'all comin' tonight? I sent you a Facebook invite."

They both nodded. Caroline pointed at my chest. "Where's your money pin?"

"I know, but I didn't think it was cool to wear for this. It's about Uncle Lionel, not my birthday."

She waved at me dismissively with the hand holding a go-cup, then handed it to Christine. "Forget that. You think he'd care about that?" She balanced her parasol under her chin and used both hands to dig through a hot pink fanny pack. She pulled out a dollar and tucked it into her bra then dug around again before locating a safety pin. "There." She pinned the dollar to my tank strap and kissed my cheek. "Happy birthday."

I smiled. I wanted to be talked into celebrating myself. "Thank you."

Christine handed the go-cup back to Caroline and pulled a dollar from her pocket. Patrick held her umbrella as she pinned the money to my chest and hugged me. "Happy birthday."

I jolted. "Oh. I took your friend's tour. Robert."

She took her umbrella back. "Good tour, right?"

"Yeah. He was great. And it was cool hearing stories about our own neighborhood. I also took the tour that goes past Robert's house."

"Really? Did they talk about it?"

She seemed concerned so I tread softly. "Yeah but they didn't use any names. It was the only house I remember them doing that. I think it was because the story ends up being about the current resident."

She nodded. "That's good."

"Hey, do you know if there's any chance his family knew my family? They lived in the same neighborhood for generations."

"Might be. I don't see why not. I can ask him. You wanna meet him? I'm actually planning to go by his place next week to pick something up. I could see if you could join me."

"That'd be great." I felt my brain exploding with questions. I would have to go home and sort out all the dates and names I already knew. I wished I had that family tree from aunt Ava's attic. The way I remembered it, all of that was recorded. Some birthplaces and biographical information were penned in later with ball point cursive. That's how we knew the chandelier story from when it still belonged to our family.

Caroline motioned toward the French Quarter. "You staying or heading back?"

I suddenly remembered. "Do you want to go see that flask now? The one at May Baily's?"

Christine closed her umbrella. "The one you wanted to see in the case when you took my tour?"

"Yeah."

She looked intrigued. "Did you figure something out?"

"You were right. The symbol on the bottom was

for my family plantation."

Her voice was excited. "Did you figure out what it was?" She looked at Caroline. "We could not figure this thing out. What did we guess? An instrument, a weapon, an insect?"

I put my hand on her arm. "It was a pump. Like for a well. Wells Plantation."

Caroline finished another sip. "And this is your family?"

"Yes. I'm just tryin' to figure some things out."

She nodded. "Let's do it. Let's go."

Patrick pulled Christine aside for a moment as I thanked Caroline and offered to refresh their drinks along the way. Then Patrick hugged and kissed me. "I'll walk back with y'all as far as the house then you guys can have some girl time."

We left him at the doorstep and headed deeper into the Quarter. It seemed like we were going closer to the river than we needed to so I interrupted our visiting to make sure we weren't just wandering.

Christine smiled and held up an envelope. "Patrick gave me this for you. And they close soon so we kinda have to hurry."

It was a gift certificate for Trashy Diva. I looked like a drowned rat and my clothes were still stuck to me, but we powered through seven selections before settling on two choices. It wasn't easy. Most of the dresses were flattering, giving and taking in all the right places for almost any female form. The girls wanted me to get the deep magenta, vintage-red-carpet "Honey Dress" because it was Pussyfooter pink. Though I was loving finding my inner pink as a Pussyfooter, I wasn't sure I wanted to bring it into the rest of my life. I ended up going with the "Obi Dress" in a large tropical flower print against a black background. It was the wide, wrapped waist that cinched it. Pun intended.

I bought a round when we arrived at May Baily's. The place was just as I'd remembered it. Dimly lit jewel tone walls and carpets housed a chocolatey wood bar and matching sturdy stools. I wandered past the photos by Bellocq. The black-and-white women were prostitutes dressed in romantic boudoir wear, posed casually. Many of the women he'd photographed seemed to have a sense of humor and almost all of them conveyed good self-esteem and a healthy dose of shamelessness.

The tone was so different from our current portrayals of prostitutes. Heck, it was different from our images of celebrities competing to see who could bare the most skin and still make the best dressed list. Sometimes when I looked into the photographic eyes of Oscar winners and ingenues posed in lingerie, or braless in dresses dropping from one shoulder, I could almost see them thinking, "For this I studied Shakespeare?" Or maybe it was just me.

It only took a Google search to find me in a halter or a bikini or owning the red carpet in basically a tissue dangling from chains. I hoped my photos were as confident and relaxed as the portraits of Bellocq's models. That amused assurance was one of my favorite things about the Pussyfooters and their uniforms. Without taking anything too seriously, the corsets and combat boots celebrated the strength of women, the power of pink. The uniforms encouraged the male gaze, but playfully and with a sense of ownership and empowerment.

My new Pussyfooter sisters motioned from the bar. We grabbed our drinks and headed over to the display cabinet. I crossed my fingers that the flask was still in there but figured Christine would've mentioned it since she still did the Brothels and Bordellos tour. I wondered if Christine still had one of those Mardi Gras rings that lit up so we could see the flask better in the dim light.

There it was. Caroline pulled out her phone, turned on some sort of bright flashlight and held it directly over the case. She clicked a photo of the silver vessel intricately carved with vines. There were a couple of dents where the patina blackened a bit.

I pointed. "The stamp is on the bottom."

We all stooped down to see better and Caroline moved her phone. Now that I knew the symbol was a well pump, it was hard to believe I never saw it before.

Christine laughed. "Of course. It's a pump. Of course it's a pump. But I wouldn't have gotten Wells from that."

"We found a bill of sale with the same symbol and it was from Wells Plantation. And there's the chandelier Lily Wells and Mama Eunoe brought with them to New Orleans."

Christine stared at the symbol. "Didn't you say something about a pipe? Was it a pipe?"

"My dad's, yeah."

Caroline took a few more photos then turned the bright light off. "I'll see if I can figure anything out. Seems like they left a few things around the city over the years. Maybe we've taken in one of their pieces before. At the very least, I can keep an eye out as new stuff comes in, let you know if I find anything."

I nodded. "That'd be great."

"And I'll send you these photos just so you have them."

We all hugged. I didn't know either of them very well but I felt great about spending my birthday with these wonderful women. "Thanks. For everything. And now I'm gonna think of y'all every time I wear this dress." I held up the signature red bag with black Chinese-font lettering.

Patrick thought the dress was beautiful. As I was holding it up and trying to show the twirl capacity of the skirt, he grabbed me and kissed me. "I love it."

"Focus. Guests are arriving in twenty minutes."

I hung the dress in the antique wardrobe and we scrambled to put out padded folding chairs and finger foods. I was still changing into my petticoat when I heard Patrick go outside to greet guests. It was kind of strange to celebrate my birthday with people I'd only known a couple of years at the most, but the only complaint I had about my new friends was that they weren't old friends. Birthdays felt like they should be about personal history somehow and these friends knew only what I'd told them – which wasn't much yet.

Like with most parties, the kitchen filled up quickly as people visited after storing beverages in the fridge. A few people sat on the chairs and ate chips and crudité in the living room, but most of us hung out on the stoop and sidewalk in front of the shotgun house. Christine and Caroline had changed into dry clothes and were joined by a couple other

Pussyfooters. Wendy and her beau came straight from dinner at Irene's so they looked more grown up than the rest of us. Like many of the guys, Patrick wore Saints gear.

Margie arrived with a musician from her band and I reminisced about a couple places in D.C. – where Margie and I were both born. It was almost like having an old friend there.

Ashley the Traffic Tranny came strutting up the street blowing her whistle. Her Tina Turner wig had to be warm in this weather. I knew this truth from wearing Sabine's pink bob in the Festigals parade. Daryl AKA Dancing Man 504 yelled, "wooooo child!" and Ashley yelled it back from half a block away. Wearing red fishnets, platform heels and shredded Daisy Dukes, Ashley was a human traffic light but she was also a "street concierge" who knew where to get things and how to connect people. She started singing *Happy Birthday* as she arrived, and everyone joined.

I looked around at all these new people in my life. Everyone seemed genuinely happy and comfortable in their own skin. No one cared that Ashley was a man or that people had paid to hear Margie earlier that night. Everyone there was a center of attention and none of them seemed to care much. It was so different than the itchy, competitive mingling people did in L.A.

Caroline showed us videos of second lines for Uncle Lionel in Norway and Sweden and we swapped stories until fireworks interrupted us. The display was meant to commemorate Bastille Day, but we liked thinking it was in honor of Uncle Lionel's spectacular life.

I threw my fist in the air. "And a celebration of Drew Brees finally signing his contract!"

"Who Dat!" Several people drank like it was a toast.

Christine lifted her go-cup. "And to commemorate the birth of Charlotte Reade!"

Everyone raised their cups as fireworks burst over the unseen river. "To Charlotte!"

Watching the red and blue flashes reflecting in the faces of the people I would spend the rest of my life becoming old friends with, I felt blessed. This was a very lucky Friday the thirteenth.

Chapter 8

The second line parades for Uncle Lionel had already gone on for two weeks owing to daily downpours. When a beloved musician passed, the other musicians played every day until the body was laid to rest – which was a weather-permitting type situation. Today's weather was no different. The rain was even more torrential than before, but the memorial ceremony went on as scheduled.

Though I hadn't attended the viewing the day before, the whole city had heard about the man "outside the box." Undertakers traveled from far away parishes to see the standing corpse of Uncle Lionel Batiste. Dressed in his typical finery with his watch across his hand, his corpse leaned slightly on a faux streetlamp, like a mannequin or a wax figure. Though I had mixed feelings about photos existing, I couldn't resist a peek at a few in my Facebook feed. Even in death, Uncle Lionel went out in style.

I donned a vibrant sundress and cute rubber sandals, my new every day footwear. I'd already accumulated four colors. I topped the ensemble with a clear, dry-cleaner-bag-type hooded rain poncho and headed for St. Charles.

The streets of the Garden District were overwhelmed. To say it was raining didn't begin to cover it. My collapsible purse-sized umbrella was flimsy against the wind and too shallow to be a shield for the sheets of water coming from all sides. Christine was already at the streetcar stop, cowering under a too-small decorative second line umbrella. We took a pass on trying to hug. Her naturally Marilyn-Monroe-white-blonde hair dripped onto her damp shoulders. The rest of her was just soaked to the skin. "Nice day for it."

I laughed. "Look at the bright side. Fewer tourists and newbies."

Christine laughed then looked at her watch. "I'm losing the faith. I've been standing here for twelve minutes. I actually thought I'd have to let one pass since I got here so early."

I looked down the empty tracks. "That's not bad."

She shook her head. "When I got here, there was a waitress heading to her shift. She said she'd been here at least twenty minutes. She ended up taking the bus."

"But don't you feel like the person who's warmed up a slot machine? I couldn't walk away over thirty minutes in." I looked down the tracks again.

Christine shouted. "Cross the street! The bus, look."

We splashed across the St. Charles and joined the other dripping riders. We all stared out the windows at the flooding in the streets. By the time we disembarked, the murky, warm water was up to the bottom step of the bus.

Bourbon Street was a canal with water flowing up onto the sidewalks and into open doors of shops and bars. Water shot geysers up through rumbling manholes. It was hard to slog through the city. By the time we crossed Rampart heading into Armstrong Park, the water was nearly knee high. This wasn't normal. The pumps couldn't be working right.

The Mahalia Jackson Theatre was packed to standing room so we were thrilled to find Caroline waving us over to saved seats. The air conditioning was cold on my wet skin and dripping hemline as I balled my hoodie into a plastic shopping bag and added my saturated umbrella.

Someone onstage explained that Uncle Lionel had time to record a few requests. His memorial was to be held in the Superdome or the Mahalia Jackson Theater. People laughed. He asked that we not wear black – unless it was Saints black and gold, of course, so the theatre was full of folks in a Crayola box of colors. He asked that we not cry. He wanted a party – a big, fun one.

I turned over the postcard someone had handed me on the way into the theatre. It read, "I'd like the memory of me to be a happy one, I'd like to leave an afterglow of smiles when life is done. I'd like to leave an echo whispering softly down the ways, of happy times and laughing times and bright and sunny days. I'd like the tears of those who grieve to dry before the sun, of happy memories that I leave behind when the day is done."

I smiled at his wish for us and flipped the card over again. The photo was of Uncle Lionel banging his drum while leaning on the back of a hearse. The card was signed, "Your New Orleans Legend, Uncle Lionel."

On the stage, Uncle Lionel's casket sat between a faux streetlamp and his iconic drum. The street signs

on the lamp were for Charbonnet and Treme. His
familiar band uniform stood with it's cap cocked to
the side, just as it had been in life.

A brass band of over fifty musicians in traditional
black and white paraded through the theatre. I spotted
members of Treme, Storyville Stompers, Young
Tuxedo and Free Agents brass bands among many
others. Given how many local bands toured during
the dog days of summer, it was an impressive display
of respect and love.

A lovely young lady did an interpretive dance to
His Eye Is on the Sparrow and several family
members and city spokesmen took the podium.
Mayor Mitch Landrieu talked about how black and
white don't make grey here, that they weave a
tapestry. I'd always thought that, like good gumbo,
this city was a stewpot where each flavor stood out
on it's own while becoming part of the whole.
Landrieu smiled at the crowd of festively dressed
locals. "We gonna be who we gonna be."

I wished Uncle Lionel could've attended the
festivities as he wanted, but it was certainly the party
he'd hoped for. There was singing, hip-swinging-ass-
smacking dancing, second line umbrellas pumping in
the air and Mardi Gras Indians in elaborately
feathered and beaded masterworks they'd spent up to
a year designing and constructing. And there were
Baby Dolls, grown women in ruffles and bloomers
carrying frilly lace and ribbon adorned parasols and
baby bottles filled with booze. Their turn-of-the-
century foremothers had inspired the founders of the
Pussyfooters. In turn, the Pussyfooters brought adult
dance groups back into the Mardi Gras tradition.

Singing, dancing and remembering Uncle Lionel with my new Pussyfooter sisters, I couldn't help but happy cry.

The organizers stalled the program as long as they could hoping the skies would clear, but the funeral ended with the announcement that the cemetery was flooded and we'd have to return Monday to try to put him in the ground. That meant four more days of second lines starting with the one led by the giant brass band that escorted us from the theatre and grew as more members outside joined. It always amazed me how musicians from all over our city, playing together for the first time, could each find moments to stand out while never losing the group's overall flavor. It was the gumbo analogy all over again, the tapestry.

We paraded through ankle-deep water in the Treme with a brief stop at the Candlelight Lounge, then up to the underpass on Claiborne. The freeway above provided a dryer path and surround-sound acoustics for our swelling crowd. I especially loved seeing the children trying out their second line dance skills – stepping and stomping, dropping into deep knee bends and hopping, then popping back up again into more skipping-like attempts at the fancy footwork.

As usual, there were people grilling barbecue or dragging coolers full of beverages for sale all along the route. When we ran out of overpass, many people headed home, especially when the rain kicked it up a notch. But dozens of diehards continued on toward the Marigny. Dancing Man 504 exchanged soppy hugs with each of us then put his fancy footwork back in motion. It didn't even seem strange to me anymore that everyone here seemed to know everyone here. I rarely had to make introductions outside of work events. We danced along together for awhile then Daryl splashed ahead with two other guys with footwork skills.

Then it really started to pour. I don't know how the musicians were able to keep playing, but as long as they did we kept pace with them as the waters rose. The strange thing was that the harder it rained, the more it energized our dancing and singing. The party continued, Caroline in tow, but Christine and I peeled off and trudged back to the streetcar stop near Canal.

Christine put a dollar and quarter into the collection machine. "I think Uncle Lionel would have been happy to see all the partying the rain delays caused."

I laughed. "All those die-hards galumphing through knee-deep floodwaters. All those musicians and paraders showing up day after day."

"It was a sendoff worthy of the man."

The Garden District wasn't as flooded as the Treme. Like the French Quarter, it was on higher ground. Robert's house looked dark and spooky inside the canopy of giant tropical plant leaves. It was easy to understand the urge to tell stories of curses about such a macabre looking place.

"Get in, get in." Robert exchanged our umbrellas for towels as he hustled us inside. "Must've been crazy out there. The pumps are down. Again."

It was as dark inside as I'd imagined. Piles of magazines and newspapers lined the foyer. More were stacked in the living room along with old hardcover books. The furniture was studded leather and dark wood from sometime in the 70's. Something his father selected?

"Can I get y'all a cool drink?"

We agreed to water and laid the towels onto the couch before sitting. The coffee table held more stacks of books, a pile of maps and a large brass bowl filled with pennies.

Robert handed us glasses of ice water and shook his hair behind his shoulders as he sat in a chair across the coffee table. "Don't let me forget the books. I have them in a bag by the door."

Christine finished a sip of water. "Thank you. I'll get them back to you in a couple weeks."

"Take your time."

She smiled. "I told Charlotte you used to do the tour that goes past her house."

Robert took me in, evaluating. "Which house is yours?"

"The one with the chandelier."

Christine's eyes went wide. "That's your family house?" We always met on the street so she'd never seen my place.

Robert smiled slightly and nodded his head in recognition. "Used to have yellow and black trim for a while. Nice house. I always liked that story."

My breath quickened. "What did you like about it?"

"There's something romantic about bringing the chandelier across the state in a covered wagon. But I like the part about giving it to their mammy after slavery ended."

"Is that why they gave it to her?"

He shrugged. "Could be."

Christine touched my arm. "Wait, do you know the secret?"

Robert pushed his hair back again. "Yes. Do tell. Have you seen it move? Was the chandelier hanging when you moved in?"

I took a breath. I knew Robert was a sceptic but he seemed pretty convinced there was a family secret worth protecting. "I think I know the secret but I don't know what it means. There's initials and a symbol on the top of the chandelier. I'm guessing the first initials are LW for Lily Wells and the next is either OW or DW but I'm guessing it's DW for Daisy Wells, Lily's sister. And the symbol is a pump, the Wells Plantation's stamp. But I can't think why that would be a secret. Any of it."

Christine offered, "Maybe they stole it and that identified where they stole it from."

I'd had that thought before. It made sense. "I'd also wondered if they changed their identity. But couldn't they have just scratched the initials and symbol off? Sanded it or something?"

Robert shifted in his cushy chair. "Maybe they were keeping the secret from the children. Maybe they didn't want the kids to know that one family owned the other family."

Christine nodded. "I could see that."

"But each generation in Sassy's family has been put in charge of making sure the chandelier is always hanging. That was when I saw it, when Taffy and UncaParis..." My brain cranked. "Wait, there was old masking tape on the top covering everything. I

95

peeked. Maybe you're right."

Christine slapped her hands up and down like they held cymbals. "Mystery solved."

Then I remembered. "I told her. I told Taffy our family owned hers and I told her to tell Chiffon." I looked to Robert. "Those are Sassy's girls, the ones that inherited the chandelier. I'm just holding onto it for them until one of them has a more suitable place to hang it."

Robert grinned slightly like it was none of his business. "It's interesting having you here in the house. Do you have a brother?"

I wasn't sure where this was going. "Yes, one. Younger."

"I suppose you already heard the lonely boy story when you took the other tour."

I nodded. Christine shifted on the towel and touched her wavy hair to see how wet it was.

Robert leaned forward onto his knees. "My family used to know your family. People in our line have babies young so our generations didn't always line up, but your great-great-grandfather and my great-great-great-grandfather were definitely friends. Oliver, right? Oliver Perry."

It felt so strange to be connected to this stranger, to feel deeply rooted in this neighborhood's stories and families. Maybe this was what it felt like to be a native. I'd moved around a lot in my life. I wasn't a native of anywhere, and I was fairly used to being the new girl. This feeling was like going to a family reunion and seeing your nose on a stranger's face. I had history and Robert was part of it somehow. "Yes, he was Lily's boy."

"Lifelong friends." Robert settled back into the leather. "In fact, my great-great-grandfather was named for him. That's why I know the story. He passed it down along with the name. I'm Oliver Robert Lafargue. My father was Oliver Reese Lafargue for his mother."

"Was your mother's maiden name Robert?"

"Yes. But the point is how lonely could he have been if he had a lifelong friend?"

Was Robert defensive or right? Either way, he didn't want me putting much stock in the Lonely Boy curse. I smiled. "Of course. Did you have to tell that story when you did the Garden District tour?"

Robert looked into the bowl of pennies. "That's why I quit." He sat forward again. "I'm a grown man. I understand that at some point you have to give up your love of history and make some money, but I couldn't do it. The owner of the tour company thought I was just being willful, but I was serious. I wanted them to remove the house from the tour. He kept pushing and pushing about me being a sceptic, about it clouding my judgement to be so close-minded. Then, like he's really onto something, he yells, 'You'd change your mind if you knew what it was like to grow up in a haunted house.'" Robert dropped his jaw dramatically. "So I say, 'I didn't. That's the point.'"

Christine and I laughed.

"Then he fired me. Lost the battle and the war. They're out there three nights a week gawking. But you must know, Charlotte."

I was busy wondering if the tour company's owner had a motive for trying to make Robert think his house was haunted. "It's not bad. It's only one guy twice a week. But I closed the front shutters the other day. The ones they could see the chandelier through."

Robert nodded. "Wise choice. I let the trees do my dirty work."

Christine laughed. "Ha! Any excuse to get out of yard work."

Robert laughed too. "True."

Christine sipped the last of her water. "Lost Emma too. His girlfriend kept doing the story knowing it wasn't really true. There wasn't any haunting or anything, just her ex's personal family history."

I nodded. "She was a guide too?"

Robert stood and grabbed his glass. "Maybe I'm unreasonable, but I couldn't get past it. She believed the curse. It blinded her. She refused to marry me the moment she heard the story so I'm not sure what the whole thing was about in the end. More water? I'm getting some."

"I'm good."

Christine handed him her glass. I waited until I heard the refrigerator door open then whispered. "Seems like both the girlfriend and the owner have reason to wanna make Robert believe in hauntings. Do you know them?"

"Yeah but--"

A top hat flew off the breakfront behind us and plopped to the floor. We froze, staring. Then I got up and walked to the cabinet. "Where'd that come from? I don't see a blank spot." I lifted onto my toes. "I can't see the top. Did that come from the top?'

Christine stared silently.

"Do we tell him? We do, right?"

Robert reentered with two waters. Since he hadn't been in the room at the time, I had to consider Robert a suspect as well. I'd already learned my lesson about not considering the victim. He handed Christine her glass and pointed to the hat on the floor. "My great-grandfather's hat. You dropped it?"

I picked it up, a little spooked to touch it. "Where does it go?"

He put his glass down and took the hat from me, placing it on top of the breakfront. As he settled back into his chair, I exchanged a look with Christine. She smiled at Robert. "Tell Charlotte about the stuff that's been happening around the house."

Robert shot her a look of surprise. I stepped in. "The chandelier really does do stuff. All kinds of things. Swaying, spinning, all the crystals sticking out like a porcupine, you name it."

Robert held my gaze. "Seriously?"

I chuckled. "My guy's never seen it. And we live together so I feel kinda crazy sometimes. Like maybe I'm tryin' to make my life more interesting. Sometimes I remind myself that I don't know everything about physics and maybe these things are possible somehow. But I can't unsee what I've seen. That's always where I land."

Robert took a sip of water. "Sometimes it's a smell. I've smelled my dad's aftershave and my aunt's perfumed talcum powder. I've heard bumps, drags. Sometimes I think they're footsteps but I remember that the brain is always attempting to matrix something recognizable, so it could just be random thumps."

I wished I could take notes without seeming odd.

He took another sip. "I've seen things move. The water has turned itself off and on when I'm in the shower. I've seen things outside too. Lights moving. Oh, and the lights go off and on sometimes. Things like that."

I didn't want to sound freaked out but that seemed like a lot of unpredictability to live with in your own home. "And this is all new? What started it?"

Robert chuckled. "The trigger. You have to know that I don't believe in any of this. I don't believe you can bring one thing into a house and the whole place suddenly has a mind of it's own. I don't believe that."

I nodded. "Sure."

"Okay. But the start of all of these goings-on lines up with when I brought home the Mason jar of marbles."

Christine jumped in. "Yes, apparently someone had stolen them from the cemetery."

I had no idea what they were talking about.

Robert took over again. "The marbles had been passed down the line, father to son. My dad played them with me a couple of times, taught me the game. A while ago I wanted to put some things behind me, so I placed the jar next to our family tomb. I figured it would get cleaned up eventually. Or maybe some kid would take the jar and put the marbles to good use. Some of them were pretty valuable but I didn't have the heart to sell them."

I thought about that. It was easier for Robert to let the marbles possibly end up in a dumpster than to sell them. People were fascinating.

Christine looked like she loved this story. "So

some tourist took the marbles home as a souvenir. They ended up mailing the jar back to the cemetery. The note said the marbles were cursed and asked that someone place them next to the family tomb again. They hoped returning the jar would stop the activity in their house."

Robert nodded. "Someone from the cemetery recognized the family name and figured I might want the marbles, so they called the tour company's office to let me know."

I was confused. "But you didn't put them back at the grave?"

He looked to Christine. "Some of my friends suggested they'd made their way home to me for a reason and that I should hang onto them."

Christine demurred. "I even suggested he put them somewhere prominent."

He laughed. "I believe the word 'shrine' came up at some point."

I was still confused. "So why not put them there now?"

Robert settled on me. "I refuse to believe this is what's happening."

I decided. "The hat was on the floor 'cause it flew off the breakfront while you were in the kitchen. Has it ever done that before? Is it secure up there?"

He looked to the hat. "The hat fell?"

Christine corrected, "Flew."

I wasn't sure I'd heard the thumps at first over our nervous laughter. Robert's expression hadn't changed. Christine jumped when the noises started again. We all looked around the ceiling. Another set of thumps and a dragging sound. I gasped involuntarily. We waited, staring at the dusty crown molding. Nothing.

I lowered my eyes. "I think it's over."

Christine took a deep breath. "What the heck was that?"

"That one's happened before. A couple of times in the last few weeks." Robert chuckled. "Honestly, I'm just glad y'all heard it too. I live alone so you never know."

I finished my water. "The chandelier seems to act up the most when I'm talking about our family history. Is there anything that seems to spark your activity?"

Robert considered for a moment. "Not that I've noticed. I'll try to pay attention to that."

Christine stood and smoothed her skirt. "Don't let me forget those books."

Robert rose and I followed. I gathered we were leaving, though it seemed abrupt.

"Thanks again." Christine hugged Robert and grabbed her umbrella.

I did the same. "Yes, thank you."

Christine pulled at the door and opened her umbrella as she stepped outside carrying the plastic bag of books. We were quiet until we latched the wrought iron gate behind us. Then Christine made an openly shocked face. "What was that? I don't know if I can go back there. That was... What was that?"

I spotted something shiny in the grass next to the gate and poked at it with my foot. It looked like a spring, about the same width as a pencil. Pretty strong little spring. Not for a pen or anything mundane. I followed Christine out from under the overhanging trees. "Seemed legit to me. But there are probably lots of ways to make that thumping noise happen. And magicians make things appear to move on their own all the time. Honestly, it could even be him doing it."

"Robert? No way. He hates all of this. But I never did like his girlfriend and I've heard his old boss is a tyrant. Another reason to love having my own company. But seriously, you think that was faked?"

Part of me really liked knowing someone else was dealing with a supernatural situation in their home. "Anything's possible."

Christine let a smile spread sideways. "Do you think the sno-ball stand is still open?"

"Hard to predict. It's not raining hard, but it's been raining all day. They might've called it."

Like grits, second lines or our casual use of brightly colored wigs, sno-balls were one of the many New Orleanian things that were nearly impossible to explain without a list of things they weren't. Sno-balls were a frozen, sweet treat but they weren't shave ice, Italian ice, gelato, sherbet, ice cream, slushies, granitas, Slurpees, popsicles and definitely not snow cones – crunchy crushed ice with near-flavorless syrup, sometimes sparsely poured in advance and frozen together in a paper cone. Awful. Sno-balls were more like fluffy snow in a cup, made to order with imaginative sock-pow flavors.

I already knew what the next topic would be – SnoWiz or Hansen's. There were many favorite sno-ball stands in the city but everything started with SnoWizard and Hansen's. Both could lay claim to inventing the confection, developing their ice-shaving technologies in the 1930's. Both were family owned and operated. Hansen's was an indoor shop decorated with photos and memorabilia in glass cases and on walls. Aproned heirs chatted with people waiting patiently in line while filling cups with shaved ice, dousing them with syrup, capping them with more shaved ice and dousing then again.

SnoWiz was a walk-up window with plastic seats facing the parking lot, but their sno-balls were about a dollar cheaper and they had more flavors including sugar-free and color-free. Their family business exploded into a worldwide distribution factory for syrups and ice-shaving machines. But sno-balls were a little like New York bagels – affected by the local water's pH content, so even a sno-ball made with genuine SnoWizard technology and syrups might not be the same as our downy dessert. Or maybe they just seemed better here because the summers were so sticky hot.

Everything dripped with sweat during the summer. Coasters and koozies were de rigueur. A soap I'd brought from L.A. perspired in the dish my first summer in the city. I wasn't sure what to make of that. My toilet tank dripped with condensation at times. I avoided bras, pants and fabric that could collect sweat stains. The windows glistened at night when we cooled down the bedroom with AC. Even now as rain drizzled down my leg, the droplets were warm, mixing with the sweat behind my knee and running down my calf without cooling it. "Yeah, a sno-ball sounds good."

Red lipstick framed Christine's smile. "Hansen's or SnoWiz?"

Chapter 9

Wendy generously offered to sell me a dress from the movie she was wrapping. She'd fit it for me if I could get downtown before lunch. Wendy was tall, easy to spot among the rolling racks.

I waved. "Hey."

"Oh hey! Great, you made it. Start on that rack there. I have a few things I pulled aside. I'll be right back." Wendy disappeared through the maze of racks as I held up the first dress then clicked through hangers, taking in each party dress. Wendy returned holding a plastic, zippered garment bag and hung it on the end of the rack, then hugged me. She pulled at the zipper. "These were the dresses for the one I said was built like you. I held them out of the sale earlier but I need to put them back in before everyone gets back after lunch."

"I really appreciate all of this."

Wendy pulled the bag off and spaced the hangers a bit on the rack. She grabbed a silver gown and spread the long skirt dramatically. "I know you said you didn't want to go long but I love this. It's a local designer."

I liked that. She knew I would. "I'll try it on but I don't want long."

She grabbed a cocktail-length silver dress and held it to her figure. "Same designer, same collection, but shorter."

The fabric was like mercury, all shimmer and fluidity. The dress didn't have much shape on the hanger and the halter top would prohibit wearing a bra. "I'm in my forties. Am I not past my braless days? Both of these are for the bold and braless."

Wendy laughed. "I fit a lot of bodies. You can still afford to go braless. I wouldn't have pulled these if I wasn't sure."

She was an expert and I did love the fabric. "Let me see some bra-friendly options and we'll see how it all plays out in the fitting room."

"I'll take it. You're easy compared to what I've been through. This last bunch was a nightmare. All A-listers like *7 Sisters*, but instead of Clarence reminding the cast and crew how much we all loved making movies, we had that overrated screaming Mimi. But it was more like Me! Me!"

I laughed. "The glamorous life."

Wendy led me to a curtained booth and unloaded the hangers onto hooks. "And it's all that exhausting stuff of everyone wanting to be someone else. I'm just not used to it anymore."

"I know, I've lost a lot of my hard-shell candy-coating too. I might melt in your hands now."

Wendy laughed. "And fame changes people. It was too many famous people together."

That assumption always bugged me. "Money, fame and power don't change people. It illuminates them, shines a spotlight on who they already are. And sure, money fame and power can be like alcohol, you can get drunk on them. But they say you never really do anything drunk you wouldn't have done sober if you were less inhibited, more fearless."

Wendy zipped the back of the first dress, a flouncy, bronze satin frock with beadwork dissipating from the shoulders. "Yeah, I sometimes feel like I'm back in school again with everyone judging stupid stuff and me not passing muster."

"But that's probably who those people were in high school, the ones you had trouble with back then. But now they have *People Magazine* covers and millions of dollars."

Wendy laughed, leading me to the nearby standing mirror. "This color is amazing with your hair. It's practically the same shade." She stepped back to take a few photos.

I did love the color. And the dress was pretty, beautiful actually. But it seemed a little generic. I clipped my hair up to showcase the beadwork but it started to feel like a pageant dress to me.

The second selection was a gold-beaded flapper-inspired dress that had to weigh at least five pounds. I always felt like I had an obligation to show my curves while I still had them at events like these. Maybe it was the pressure of doing red carpets next to surgically-perfected demigods with personal trainers and home gyms. I liked to think it was the Pussyfooter in me, the woman willing to try parading through her own city in a pink corset and wig.

The dresses were all lovely – tasteful and finely detailed, but I still hadn't found "the one." Only the silver choices were left. I took off my "set bra" – a nude, seamless, padded number, and dropped it on top of my rubber sandals. I knew I wouldn't be choosing the gown so I tried it first. Wendy helped me figure out the halter straps then smiled. "Wow."

I held the hem up and walked to the mirror. I was stunning. "Holy cow."

"Oh Charlotte, please, please, please consider wearing this. You owe it to the dress. It was made for you."

I stared at the shimmering tower in the mirror. "It's my first choice for the Oscars I won't be attending."

"It'll probably get nominated for something though, don't you think?"

"*7 Sisters*? I would assume so. But I won't be going either way, so this is beautiful but way over the top for the occasion." I took one last look. "It is amazing though." Wendy took her photos and I headed back to the fitting room for my last hope at perfection. I could see it on Wendy's face even before I returned to the mirror.

She fixed the ballet-slipper-inspired black laces around my ribs and waist and smiled again. "You're crazy if you don't wear this."

I turned to face myself and instantly agreed, braless breasts and all. I liked when my red carpet choices combined classic with something daring, something bold. This backless liquid-silver, knee-length, halter dress checked my boxes. "Done. Talk me into it, but done."

"No talking. You're done. Gotta get these back out on the floor real quick. I'll go look up the price. Do you mind if I send a photo to Lisa, the designer?"

I pulled the dress off and reset my bra. "Of course. Tell her I love it. And write her name down for me so I have it memorized for the carpet."

After I changed, I carried the winning dress to Wendy texting on her phone. She looked up. "Lisa would love for you to wear the dress. You just made her day. And I looked it up. We're supposed to return her dresses to her. So, it's yours for the event."

"Really? That's amazing." I gave Wendy a big hug.

"Yeah, and she's thrilled to lend it to you. We didn't end up using her pieces in the show so a red carpet is a pretty big deal for her."

"So you made two people's day."

Wendy handed me a bag for the dress. "Which makes my day."

"Oh, I forgot to tell you. I went to Robert's house."

"The tour guide? What were you doing there? What'd you think of his place? A little frozen in time. And I wouldn't say hoarder, but he's definitely crossed the line on collector."

"A top hat flew off a breakfront while we were there. And we heard thumping. An undeniable quantity of thumping."

She finished hanging the last of the dresses on their designated racks. "Seriously? Was it scary?"

"A little. Confusing mostly. Can you think of any reason Robert would want people to think his house is haunted?"

Wendy shook her blonde, layered waves. "He hates ghost tours, says they're all lies. He says the story of his house is a lie and anyone who knows him and tells it is a liar."

"Sounds pretty heated about the whole thing."

She chuckled. "Hot and bothered. He's dead serious. He dumped his girlfriend over it."

"I heard." Which meant he was telling the truth about that. His truth, which could be warped by his perspective that believing in the curse made you a traitor. At the very least it meant you were "blinded," as Robert would say. But it was hard to think of a reason Robert would want people to think his house was haunted. He genuinely seemed to hate the attention the house already received. That jungle obscuring his windows took decades to grow. He seemed pretty invested in being taken off the tour. No, he didn't appear to have any kind of motive. Though he did have access. And knowledge of what makes a good ghost story. But no, it didn't make sense so it probably wasn't him. "And quit his job, right?"

Wendy held up her I'm-making-a-point finger. "Got fired. So fired. Everyone heard about it."

"Did that hurt him tryin' to find new work?"

"Yeah, but not really. Everyone knows he's worth the occasional hissy fit he's bound to throw."

"Except the guy who fired him."

"Lou. Yeah. He can be a jerk though. People know that, too."

I wanted to believe that I wasn't the only person in the neighborhood dealing with supernatural stuff, but it did seem like there were a couple of bridges Robert had burned. Or maybe it was about money. Maybe the owner, Lou, wanted to add new material to boost sales and saw an opportunity to kill two birds with one haunted object story. And there was always the woman scorned. "Do you believe anyone who marries Robert is doomed? I would think that would make it tough to be his girlfriend."

"Emma was never a perfect fit. I think she used the curse to keep her options open. He's always talking about her being blinded, but it's that whole love-is-blind thing that I think really got him. He should start with the man in the mirror. He never wanted to see how much she wanted to control him. He saw it as her being a strong woman who knew what she wanted."

We walked toward the elevator together. "Did she get over the break-up? How long ago was it?"

Wendy shrugged. "Two years? I heard she had a boyfriend at some point. They've already done all that stuff where you run into each other on a date, or whatever horrors you have to get past to get on with life."

"Do you think his house really could be haunted?"

She pushed the down-arrow button. "Remember Irene Sage at French Quarter Fest?"

"The bees!"

"Yes, we're all there at the Coco Robicheaux memorial concert and that gigantic swarm of tens of thousands of bees showed up."

I could see it clearly. "They formed like a funnel, a tornado-like swirl in the middle of the crowd. And no one panicked. That was kinda the weirdest part."

"And no one seemed to get stung either."

"And they didn't seem to come from anywhere and then they just dissipated after a couple songs. It was one of the most remarkable things I've ever seen."

Wendy smiled. "Irene said it must be Coco up to his old Voodoo tricks. Did you believe her?"

I smiled back as the elevator dinged its arrival. "I have no better explanation."

We hugged and I headed back out into the bustling French Quarter. A brass band played *Little Liza Jane* on the corner. A guy in an alligator costume walked toward me with a hand puppet of a an old man covering his right arm. The gator-man's spiked tail swayed as he leaned over to check on a drunk on the sidewalk. You never knew what you were going to see here.

I used to hate leaving New Orleans. Every time I got back on a plane, it felt like I was being torn from my mother's arms. I often cried long and hard enough to generate concern among my fellow passengers. Sometimes I still realized I lived here now – I wouldn't have to leave, and I'd fill to bursting with happiness. Watching the alligator man exchange a shrug with his puppet and walk off to the beat of corner music, I was having another one of those moments.

I liked that I walked more now. I liked only dialing seven numbers on the phone. I liked that I hardly ever carried a purse anymore. I'd always been more of a city girl. I liked that costumes were normal here and elective surgery wasn't. I liked that most of the city's events were open to the public, not tucked behind velvet ropes guarded by clipboard-carrying bouncers.

Certain types of street performers went in and out of vogue over the years. One-man-bands were overtaken by breakdancers by the late 80's. There were still plenty of kids tapping with Coke cans smashed under their sneakers, but lately I'd noticed bucket drummers – kids banging on overturned plastic paint drums. And there was free music everywhere. Brass bands were still the staple but a the new thing seemed to be bands dressed like Dexy's Midnight Runners playing twangy music on banjoes and washboards. The men almost always had beards usually reserved for religious zealotry and a hat of some sort.

As I was passing one of those bands, the guy in front of me stopped his girlfriend and said with deep reverence, "This is jazz." I was all for the guy stopping to appreciate the music, but it was ragtime. I had no idea where ragtime was born. The guy pulled out his phone to take a photo. I wasn't sure why it irritated me that this couple would go home thinking this was local music played by local musicians. But it did.

I'd been putting off calling Taffy, but Patrick wasn't home from work when I returned. I pulled a bag of carrots and a cucumber out of the refrigerator and grabbed the peeler before dialing.

Taffy was laughing when she picked up. "Y'all calm yourselves and wash up for supper. Stop teasin' Jojo or we leavin' him outside until he can calm hisself." She shut a door and laughed again. "They had the sprinkler out. Remember when runnin' through the sprinkler was like Disneyland without all the lines? But now the dog's all riled up. Not his fault. Fun overdose. What's goin' on with you?"

"This is gonna be one of those weird conversations."

Taffy clanked a big spoon inside a pot. "A quick weird conversation, I hope. I got supper comin' up in about five."

I had a considered explanation but jumped into the thick of things. "It's possible I may have made a mistake telling you about the Wells family owning Lottie."

She stopped stirring the pot. "What kind of mistake?"

"What if that was the secret Mama Heck was protecting? What if she always wanted the chandelier to hang so you'd never see the stuff etched into the top?"

Taffy was quiet for a moment. "I don't know. Mama seemed pretty adamant about it hanging, like she knew the secret."

"Then why don't you know it? Shouldn't Sassy have passed it down to you? But if the idea was to keep the secret from the children, it would make sense no one ever told you the secret, right? Maybe your mom didn't know it either. Maybe she just took the job of protector very seriously."

"So I shouldn't tell my children? Don't you think Mama woulda mentioned somethin' like that?"

"Maybe she figured you couldn't tell what you didn't know."

Taffy's kids came back into the kitchen and her voice got louder. "Okay Charlotte, well it was good to hear from you. I won't be spreading any manure on the garden anytime soon, but thanks for the heads up."

Why didn't Taffy and Chiffon know the secret? Had I blown it by telling them about the bill of sale? Was that even the secret? How could we be sure we were protecting the secret if we weren't sure what it was? I couldn't help but feel I'd somehow botched things.

Chapter 10

Patrick turned on the TV we almost never used in the bedroom and woke me. "It's Hubig's."

The news video was of a building entirely engulfed in flames during the night. Hubig's Pies was an institution. Fried hand-pies filled with apple, lemon curd, chocolate, peach or sweet potato – the small, neighborhood factory had been in operation nearly a century. "That's terrible. Maybe people will pitch in to rebuild it like they did with Verti Marte."

"I just hope someone hires the forty employees. I'm sure the building and business were insured." Patrick leaned in for a kiss. I loved that it was his first instinct to worry about the people. It made him perfect for the job of protecting the French Quarter and it's history. He smiled. "It's time to get up."

I wasn't much of a morning person. It didn't help that I wasn't a coffee drinker. I preferred the slow, steady burn of a high-protein breakfast. But I rallied. Patrick was so kind to have taken the day off to pick up Mom and my stepdad, Joe, from the airport. It was a true sacrifice for someone who loved his job as much as Patrick did.

I was surprised to find him making breakfast, bacon and eggs. I didn't remember buying bacon. He must've planned this. A bouquet of flowers sat on our living room table. Was this still about my birthday?

Patrick had already been so generous. Was it our anniversary?

"Oh hey. It'll be a few more minutes."

I smiled. "What's going on? This is wonderful."

Patrick took my hand and sat me on the couch. He smiled.

I smiled.

"I love you."

"I love you too."

"This is everything I ever wanted. You are everything I ever wanted."

My heart started banging against my ribs.

His eyes got glassy. "I just want to do this forever." He pulled a box from his pocket. "I want to be your husband and I want you to be my wife. Will you marry me?"

I couldn't see the ring through my tears. "Yes."

We hugged and I felt free somehow. So many things felt so clear. After all of those years of railing at the wind about my horrifying dating life, it was clear that none of it was wasted. All of it led to this moment with this man. After enduring so much confusion and pain, everything was crystalline.

I'd sometimes been afraid Patrick was a player when we met. He seemed too good to be true, like he'd read my wish list and was luring me in by pretending to be a gentleman, hard worker and ethical person. I realized it made more sense for him to pretend to be something flashier than a good guy, but I'd been fooled before. There was always that danger when dating people known for their acting abilities and/or ability to read people. And L.A. and I never agreed on the rules of courtship – or that there was

:h a thing as courtship.

Kissing my future husband for the first time, I as so grateful I hadn't let myself become embittered and shut down. To say it wasn't easy would be a laughable understatement. The culture of L.A. could be downright treacherous to the soul. Even dating people outside of my industry didn't seem to help much. My last two years there, I became genuinely worried over how much damage had been done. I made a concerted effort and developed daily habits to keep a doorstop in my heart.

I did what I called "spiritual dancing" at least two nights a week. It mostly consisted of me moving and grooving in my living room while picturing myself feeling exactly the way I was feeling right now. Because of my career, I knew that you could create an emotion by mimicking actions and reactions connected to that emotion – if you looked over your shoulder enough times when you were walking down the street, you'd actually start to get scared someone was following you. So, I mimicked the emotions of feeling happy, safe and carefree enough to dance, enjoy my body moving and feel loved.

I listened to the same song every night before my prayers, allowing myself to believe it was from my partner to me. I visualized him being out there somewhere wondering what was taking me so long to show up. And I let myself believe, even if only for those moments, that my past was no indication of my future – that I really just hadn't met the right guy yet.

I was dedicated and steadfast with my routines for those years. It was enough. My heart was banged-up but beating strong. I felt electric.

The bacon started popping and Patrick went to attend it. "Sorry, I know we're on the clock. I planned this a couple of times but the one thing I knew I wanted was for your mom to be here."

I felt so known. "Really?"

"I knew she'd be the first person you'd want to tell and I wanted her to be able to be here for that. I even thought of proposing at the airport so you wouldn't have to wait to tell her, but now everyone has cameras on their phones. You know how I feel about people taking my picture."

"This is perfect."

For years, my mother had awaited my arrival at various gates in the New Orleans airport. It was still funny to me that now I awaited her flights. As was sometimes the case, a brass band played in the terminal. As always, the smell of Cafe du Monde beignets greeted us as we headed to meet Mom and Joe. Our airport was fairly old but had to be more welcoming than any other.

It was easy to spot Mom's beaming smile and waving hand in the back of the exiting crowd. Everything felt like it was taking too long. Mom had been such a warrior for me in those rough-and-tumble years. She'd always been my mom when I was a kid, but we'd become true friends as adults. She'd listened to painful stories of people hurting her child and was able to talk about it woman-to-woman. She added me to her church's prayer chain. And she supported my continued search for the "right guy" without judgement for the many times I'd been wrong.

I remembered when we first talked about Patrick

being the right guy. It was actually Mom who said it. I was worried it might all go away and she said, "Nope. I'm taking myself off-duty. I'm switching to praying for your continued happiness." I knew she was right. I hated it that I still had nagging doubts that had nothing to do with Patrick. So I laughed and said, "Alert the prayer chain."

Mom broke from the crowd and we all exchanged hugs as Joe started talking about luggage. I couldn't wait any longer. I popped my hand up in front of my mother and waited for the solitaire ring to register. She smiled, then looked quizzical then gasped. "Oh! Oh! You're engaged? Oh!" She grabbed me and hugged me again then went for Patrick. Joe hugged me and said we should pick up some champagne on the way to the house.

We caught up on the trip to aunt Ava's. Most of the journey was the Causeway, the longest bridge-over-water in the world. With no suspensions blocking our view and only a low guard rail between drivers and Lake Pontchartrain, it felt like boating – like we were flying tall across the surface of the water. Lucky commuters could be treated to an entire sunset during the half-hour-ish drive. But we would be at Ava's by lunch.

The baby-faced burly guy at the gate waved us into the neighborhood. Though they'd lost over 300 trees in The Storm, the trees surrounding the houses were lush and live oaks still dipped over the roads. We pulled into the crowded drive and walked through the unlocked front door.

Voices emanated from the kitchen sitting room and we followed them as Mom yelled out, "Woo hoo!

We're here." Lillibette was bustling around the kitchen, preparing our serve-yourself meal. Aunt Ava sat regally in her high-backed chair. We took turns leaning in to hug her then hugged May, my cousin Tate, and the rest of the gang.

I spotted a bottle of champagne on ice and a cake on a crystal pedestal. At first I thought it was a birthday cake. Our family could easily stretch a birthday into a birth-month. But, the top of the cake read "Congratulations." Clearly Patrick had called ahead. I loved him even more.

Lunch was delicious. Shrimp-remoulade-stuffed tomatoes, boudin balls, dirty rice, cornbread, stuffed mushroom caps, spinach and strawberry salad and melba toast with a brie and lump crabmeat dip. I ignored the mushrooms and got seconds and thirds of the crab dip.

The rule was that whoever cooked didn't clean so I'd normally jump in, but everyone agreed I should relax. I hated to trouble Lillibette but hopefully she'd remembered my request for the photo album with the family tree. "Did you get a chance to go up to the attic?"

Lillibette exhaled.

"Don't worry about it. I can get it. Can you narrow down where it might be?"

"Tate, could you--"

"Of course." He finished refreshing his drink and motioned for me to follow him to the elevator.

The attic was huge, but the roof sloped sharply on either side. I hoped the album wasn't under the part where I invariably hit my head. "Do you know where it is?"

"Should be with the family things." We passed my pile, shoved deep under the eaves when I first moved south and found how much more stuff I had than storage. It was mostly books and memorabilia in boxes and large plastic tubs. Tate motioned with his glass. "I wanna say the photo albums are not far from the Christmas decorations since they make their way downstairs at about the same rate of speed. The tree's over here."

I followed him past Lillibette's overflow from her post-Storm relocation and Maw Maw's old pedal-driven sewing machine. The tree boxes were stacked next to labeled boxes of ornaments and decorations. Though it was a giant chore, I'd always loved helping the cousins decorate when I was in town.

Tate opened the top drawer of a large bureau, then the next. "Which one is it?"

I walked over and took in the stacks of photo albums in the drawer. "It's got a black cover with gold lettering. I forget what it says. Probably 'photo album.'"

We stood shoulder-to-shoulder and went through the albums, stacking them on top of the bureau. When the drawer was empty, Tate closed it so we could check the next one. We replaced the albums from the last drawer before going through the next batch. I was only on my second album when Tate held up a black one.

"I think that's it. Open it."

He raised the cover revealing the family tree written on a piece of yellowed paper. He handed the album to me.

"Can I take this? Or take a photo of this? That's actually all I really need. Yeah, I don't want to worry anyone with me taking it anywhere. Do you have a camera on you?"

He reached into his back pocket and handed me his phone. I took a few shots and emailed them to myself then returned the phone. Tate smiled. "That's it? You're good?"

"Great."

It didn't occur to me until after we were on the elevator that the family might've enjoyed going through one of Maw Maw's old albums. It was just as well since everyone was gathering drinks and snacks for the boat when we returned.

We spent the afternoon taking a leisurely trip on the river, waving at water skiers and kneeboarders, nibbling stilton cheese and crackers, listening to the Neville Brothers and Dr. John and enjoying each other's company.

It was hard saying goodbye to everyone but we apparently had reservations for a just-the-two-of-us dinner at Commander's Palace back in the city. During the car trip back across the Pontchartrain, Patrick and I finally got a minute alone to giggle about becoming engaged. He was so right about me wanting to be with my mom for that moment. And about letting my family celebrate with us. I loved how he focused on the heart of the matter.

Commander's was easily one of my favorite restaurants in the world – and I'd eaten my way across a fair stretch of the planet. One of the oldest restaurants in the city, it was the birthplace of the "celebrity restaurant chef" having launched the careers of Paul Prudhomme and Emeril Lagasse. Tory McPhail was the current genius-in-chief.

When I was in high school, I'd come up with a mantra – my dreams are alive and becoming my reality. Having just spent the day with my family, sitting in this award-winning restaurant across from the man I'd dreamed might be real, I knew this was everything I needed to be happy.

Then I understood another reason why people in L.A. avoided committed relationships. This kind of happiness was worth protecting from my industry. It was worth giving up the appearance of being available, knowing that might affect my casting. It was worth avoiding travel and prolonged separations. This kind of happiness was satiating. Showbiz thrived on ambition and hunger. I was suddenly glad Patrick and I hadn't met earlier in life. I was proud of my work and the drive and tenacity it took for me to create my career. I was glad I didn't have to choose between ferociously forging my path in the industry and being happy and loved. I had the resumé now to relax a little about proving myself. And love wasn't late finding me, it had given me a couple of decades to have a career that was hard on relationships.

Co-proprietors Ti and Lally came by the table and congratulated us as we waited for our meal. It was rare for us to see them both there. The cousins were always lovely, dressed impeccably with welcoming smiles and witty conversation. I particularly liked Ti's tiny-studded loafers. They looked like something royalty would wear around the castle, comfortable and luxurious. Both women admired my new Trashy Diva dress.

It was in season so I had the soft shell crab. That was pretty much a rule for me – if they were serving soft shell crab, I was ordering it. Same with the Ponchatoula Strawberry Shortcake, Patrick's favorite thing that might appear on the menu. The gorgeous stack of giant golden biscuit, sliced strawberries and Chantilly whipped cream arrived on a plate inscribed in chocolate script, "Congratulations."

Chef Tory came by the table as we were scraping whipped cream and strawberry juice from the empty plate. I was wise enough to know how spoiled I was about food. My father was a self-taught, at-home gourmet chef so I'd grown up on Coq au Vin and brandied Cornish game hens as well as both my parents' traditional southern dishes. Even as a small child, my mom and dad had taken me to nice restaurants on occasion. I knew what maitre d's and hors d'oeuvres were long before I knew there was no Santa. And thanks to my career, my fancy friends and my kooky dating life, I'd eaten in some of the finest restaurants known to the human palate.

But I had the good sense to know that I was living a rare life. Sure, I'd been on the hot-lunch program, eaten government cheese and even lived in my car briefly in my up-and-down life, but I'd had an amazing adventure from the start. Still, I felt humbled that Chef Tory took the time to visit with us, even as he made it so easy to just be friends discussing stuff around the neighborhood. We gushed about the meal. He told us about the blueberries that would be coming in soon and we promised to be back.

The walk home was almost stereotypically magical. Streep lamps illuminated the historic homes and mansions. The sweet olive was in bloom, filling the air with invisible clouds of intense, citrus-honeysuckle perfume – my favorite smell in the the plant kingdom. Even the rat running along the phone line ahead of us seemed like it should be singing *Down in New Orleans* from Disney's *The Princess and the Frog*. Patrick and I held hands and talked about good food – and everything seemed right with the world. I tried not to let that panic me, to not worry about how long it would last or how hard it would be to lose. Instead, I held my man's hand and enjoyed our beautiful neighborhood with a Trashy-Diva-covered belly full of delicious crab and strawberries, my favorite foods.

Patrick laughed when I asked if he was happy. "Happy? I'm the happiest. Best day ever."

"Thank you for all the effort. You really thought about what would make me happy."

He laughed again. "You should get a turn once in a while. I know fairies don't do my laundry and meals don't magically appear. Dishes get done, floors get mopped, you do all of that stuff just because it has to get done."

"Well, and I'm often unemployed."

Now he really laughed. "You're the hardest working unemployed person I know. You would be well within your rights to go on strike until I pitched in more."

These were the type of conversations I got to have now. "You handle our schedule and all of our travel. That's huge for me. Trust me, I have few complaints."

He pulled his keys out as we approached the door to our unit. "I have complaints, but they're like – oh, the martini maker in my car is broken."

I laughed and we kissed before he pushed the door open.

Chapter 11

I checked my email as I waited for the toast to pop, my new engagement ring glinting in the morning sun. A bunch of junk and one from Christine saying that Robert had experienced more activity in the house. She wanted to know if I was around for brunch. I wrote yes, hit send, then opened the email from WWLTV confirming my parking and studio entry details for today's interview.

I'd done plenty of interviews in my life but most had been on a red carpet, not on a couch in front of a camera crew. Security led me quietly down a long hallway and through the stage door. He deposited me in the small holding area with self-serve coffee and some chairs. I could see a familiar, local news face exchanging banter with a chef behind a well-lit kitchen counter. The chef explained her steps as Eric Paulsen made his way from the news desk area in the back toward a pleasantly decorated couch area closer to me. He settled in and someone checked his mic.

A smiling young woman peeked into the holding area. "Charlotte?"

I smiled back. "Yes."

"You're up after the band and the next segment."

I stood so she could find a place for the mic-pack and somewhere to clip the mic. Over her shoulder, the chef offered a plate of some festive-looking dish to the familiar-face guy and they both took bites. As they mmmm'ed over the food, the Soul Rebels began to play. I loved that it was totally normal here to have a funky brass band kick off the day on the morning news show. They played us out to commercial and the crew moved everything into place for the next segment. Sally-Ann Roberts took her place on the couch next to Eric and crossed her long legs. She had a Miss America smile and was clearly a pro, but seemed accessible and entirely genuine.

As we came back from commercial, the duo bantered then jumped into a discussion of the latest event at the Convention Center. I focused on my notes, running through everyone's names and attaching an anecdote to each person. People seemed to like behind-the-scenes stories of their favorite actors. But nearly every interview I'd done for a decade included some question about what it was like to work with Clarence, so I started there. I wanted to make sure I chose a story that really spoke to the question – what was it like? And the implication – how was it different than working with other noteworthy directors?

But I really had no idea what we'd talk about. That was always the scary part about live interviews. Miss Sally-Ann talked about the Soul Rebels' regular Thursday gig at Les Bon Temps Roule. I'd gone a few times not long after moving here and was blown away by the band's talent and energy. They made it impossible not to dance. The band played my favorite of their originals, *504*. It impressed me that they finished the entire song before we went to commercial. It was given equal time to an entire segment.

When we went off-air again, Sally-Ann stood to clear the couch for me. She extended her hand. "Congratulations on the movie. We all can't wait to see it." Her smile was energizing, like vitamin C. She stepped off the riser as Eric stood to greet me and congratulate me as well. Sometimes during the small talk before an interview, you could tell if the person did homework on you or would just be reading questions from the teleprompter. We got on the topic of parades and I told him I'd joined the Pussyfooters. Eric seemed so genuinely interested in my little reveals that I wasn't sure if he was a fan of my work or just really good at his job.

Someone counted us back in and Eric and I both looked toward the teleprompter covering the lens of the camera. The short montage I'd emailed the producer was playing on the monitor.

Eric waited for his cue. "We're here with local actress Charlotte Reade, star of the upcoming Clarence Pool movie, *7 Sisters*."

I made my usual joke about not being a star in a cast like that and assumed we'd do the normal interview dance. But then he talked about me not having been born here and let me talk about my parents meeting at L.S.U. and returning to my family home in time for the Saints to win the Super Bowl. I started to understand that his audience might not have the usual questions, they might want to know more about me as a member of the community.

Eric's bright blue eyes glinted. "And you've recently become a member of the Pussyfooters."

"Yes. I just did my first parade but it was a second

line. I haven't done one with floats yet."

As Eric moved the conversation to *7 Sisters*, it became clear he'd looked into me. Either that or he knew my work. He made it easy to see where he thought my answers could go while asking very open-ended questions. It was more of a fun dance with a good leader willing to let me twirl as opposed to the usual lead-and-follow.

He laughed when I called the movie "a rock 'em, sock 'em 70's action sister flick with fencing, martial arts, explosions, award-worthy dialogue and inclusive casting." He asked if I'd auditioned here and opened an opportunity for me to say Clarence had written the part with me in mind. Then we danced into Hollywood South and I got to brag about having state-of-the-art facilities, the first green studio and seasoned local cast and crew.

Eric wrapped things up with the release date and I did the dreaded relaxed-smile-into-the-camera while feeling time slow down. Finally, the red light went off and I genuinely relaxed and smiled as Eric and I thanked and complimented each other.

Christine was waiting outside the Ruby Slipper when I finished the interview. I'd had to cross the entire Quarter diagonally to get there but I'd eaten at the Mid-City location once and it was worth the two hour wait I'd put into the experience. But that was back when it wasn't normal for me to eat amazing southern cuisine all the time. Now I was hoping she'd put our name on the list before popping outside.

I waved and she looked instantly relieved, yelling from across the street, "We're up!"

Serendipity. I ordered the Eggs Cochon Benedict

– pork debris cooked overnight with an apple braise then piled on top of a beyond delicious hamburger-bun-sized buttermilk biscuit topped with poached eggs and hollandaise sauce. It was divine. I might never try another dish on the menu.

I told Christine about the engagement and showed her the ring. But she hadn't gotten through my single days with me and she'd met Patrick, so there wasn't much to tell. As a new friend who'd only known me happily partnered with Patrick, Christine could be a new kind of friend for me, one who met me when I was prioritizing happiness, the post-leap-of-faith Charlotte. That could be interesting and fun in ways I hadn't experienced since my leap into a career in acting. I was so glad I'd met Patrick post-leap. He met the version of me that was trying to be strong, not tough. I didn't need to be showbiz-tough most of the time anymore. I could afford to just be strong.

I had to ask. "So what happened to Robert?"

Christine finished a sip of her Bloody Mary. The Ruby Slipper's motto was, "You can't drink all day if you don't start in the morning." She blotted her lips with a napkin. "A bunch of stuff. He heard that thumping again. There was some kind of scratching noise in a wall. His chair smelled of his aunt's powder. That's the kind of detail that a tour guide would turn into a story about his aunt not wanting him to marry."

"What's with the marbles? And what would they have to do with the aunt? Seems more like a Dad thing. They were passed down father to son."

"Right."

I smiled. "But he left them at the cemetery 'cause

he wanted to put some things behind him. Maybe he wanted to put the father-son-passing-thing behind him, end the curse. Maybe he secretly believed his aunt and left the jar after she passed to symbolically end that." I switched gears. "Assuming it's all fake like he hopes, I'm tryin' to think who might want to make Robert think his house is haunted. The girlfriend was apparently pretty invested in her beliefs. And she was probably angry he basically dumped her 'cause he saw her as disloyal and ridiculous. The tour owner, Lou, basically admitted he believed he'd grown up in a haunted house and was also angry at Robert. Plus, he has the added bonus of potentially gettin' something out of it financially. More ghost stories means more money."

Christine nodded. "Well, I've met them both and neither is the pillar of stability. I could see either one of them being cruel in this way if it served them. And money makes a good motivator."

"But it seems like the whole thing requires some skill. Gettin' in the house undetected and manipulating things unnoticed. Once you're in the house, it's easy enough to apply a scent to a chair but the thumping and objects moving, that takes rigging. That takes mechanics or wires or somethin'. Maybe even electricity and timers. Maybe an electrician? An inventor?"

Christine took a stab. "A magician?"

"A special effects person." My phone rang and I meant to silence it, but accidentally sent the call to voice mail. I checked the number. Claudia. "It's my agent. I'll call her back after we eat."

I did and Claudia told me I had a table reading of Reuben's movie. I asked if they'd gotten the money yet.

She answered in her amused gargled-with-gravel voice. "He's always managed to get it done somehow. And apparently the reception went well. His buddies that own a car lot loved you."

Ah, that was probably who Victor and Jernard were. I was doubly glad I'd met them first and found them again at the end. I took down the date and time then changed into loose short-shorts and house slippers. I'd been waiting patiently since yesterday for this moment. I opened my computer and clicked the photo of the family tree.

The phone rang. Sofia. "Hey! I'm so glad you called. I have amazing news."

"You're getting married!"

I laughed. "I'm gettin' married! I forgot we had that mind-meld thing sometimes. You should totally have guessed I got a great part. That's every other call I've ever made to you that started with 'I have amazing news.'"

I told her about how Patrick asked and that he wanted me to be able to tell my mom face to face. That gesture meant so much to me and Sofia knew that the way an old friend would. "I love the way that marriage is sexy here. Most people want to be married or perma-paired somehow and I've even seen guys make fun of each other here for not having a girlfriend or a wife, like it speaks poorly of you somehow."

Sofia laughed. "Doesn't it though? I mean it says no one can put up with you or you're ridiculously picky.

I laughed. "Or you're just really unattractive."

Sofia laughed harder. "And have no money."

I was laughing too. I loved when we got like this. "But guys in L.A. are terrified of being coupled. They didn't even like it if you said the word 'dating' when that was clearly what you were doing."

She was snort-laughing now. "I'm so hot, I'm totally incapable of being in a family."

"Sleep with me. I'm disinterested in sharing my life."

Sofia was cry-laughing. "Let's have sex. I hate babies."

I laughed too. "Aw, that's rough. But mostly true." I settled. "I'm so glad I'm not in that anymore."

Though I could tell she was trying to be serious, Sofia was still laughing. "You did it." She tried to pull it together. "Charlotte, you did it, you found him."

"I did. After all of that, I really did."

We chatted for awhile about Nia's new love for Barbies and Mark's latest sculpture showing. We got back onto Patrick and I thanked her for always being there for me during those years. "I know it wasn't always fun or easy."

"We made it fun."

"That's why I'm thanking you."

Talking to Sofia always left me in a better place but I was kind of glad when we hung up. I'd waited long enough to look at this family tree. I fired up the laptop and focused.

At the top were Iris Taylor and Homer Wells. Next were Lily, Daisy and their brothers. Lily branched off with Leonard Oliver Perry and had Oliver Wells Perry. I stopped to picture Oliver playing with Robert's ancestor, running around the neighborhood when the streets weren't paved and many of the houses hadn't been built yet. I pictured them playing marbles, squinting, tongue bit to the side as they zeroed in on some prized target. Since Robert's family names were either French or Creole, I had to wonder if his family had seen mine as those crass Americans who'd taken over. Maybe they saw our family as gentrifiers or whatever their version of a New Dat might have been.

I focused on the tree again. Oliver married Ruby Smith and had my grandmother, and I knew the rest. So all I'd really learned was the names of Lily's parents, the owners of the Wells Plantation. I read the ballpoint note near Lily's name. "Lily was disowned for marrying overseer. Ran to Texas with family chandelier." Family chandelier. I wasn't sure what to make of that. Did that mean the chandelier was their only one or that this one meant more to the family than others in the home? Or was it a detail added without thinking? Maybe it meant nothing.

I felt a bit deflated. I'd hoped the tree would reveal something revelatory, or at least new. I went back to the top and took it all in again. Iris and Homer, Lily and Leonard, Daisy marries Leonard Bird Wells. Wait, what? Leonard Bird Wells?

My hand was shaking as I searched for the photo my brother had sent of our dad's family tree. I double-clicked. There it was, Leonard Bird Wells, my father's grandfather. Married to Daisy Wells, her maiden name. That must've been a seriously common surname for her to have married someone with the same last name. Maybe they were cousins. That happened more frequently back then.

Whether is was coincidence or being cousins that brought them together, I was related to myself. Daisy was both my great-great-grand aunt on my mom's side and my great-grandmother on my dad's side. Tate was going to flip. I sat with it for a moment. Realizing my parents' families had married before, I felt destined somehow, like I was meant to be born. As a child of divorce, it made me feel good to think my parents were meant to marry. But it was also pretty weird.

The chandelier jostled in our bedroom. I yelled down the hall. "Hey Mama Heck. Or Mama Eunoe? Sassy? Is this the secret? I'm my own cousin?"

I was joking, of course. Mama Eunoe stayed with Lily, Leonard and Oliver long after Daisy left. I couldn't imagine the secret had much to do with Daisy other than her initials possibly being inscribed in the chandelier.

The jostling became a rattle and I ran down the hall to catch the chandelier in action. I rounded the door entry and slid to a startled stop. The crystals were lifting up and dropping down in waves.

The undulation was still going when Patrick walked in the door trying to jiggle his key out of the old lock. "Hey."

"Come quick! Hurry!"

He didn't so I ran to him and urged him to the door, pointing to the chandelier. "Look!"

He did, but the crystals were gently swinging to a stop. "What?"

I shook my head in defeat. "Never mind."

"Love you anyway."

"But you think I'm seeing things."

He smiled. "We all believe what we need to."

I shot the chandelier a nasty look and told myself it was only a matter of time before Patrick saw it do its thing.

Chapter 12

Preseason was normally the time of year where football teams tried out their new players to see who would make the cut. But I was learning the Saints almost never did things "normally." Between the much ballyhooed bounty scandal and the eternal negotiation for Drew Brees' contract, we'd had a long, worrying off-season. With head coach Sean Payton out for the season and acting head coach, Joe Vitt, out for six games, the Saints would not only be testing out players, they'd also be testing out coaches.

The stench of misconduct hung in the air where former defensive coordinator Gregg Williams once stood. And many of our defensive players would be sitting out for up to half the season. You would've thought Saints fans would be disinterested or downtrodden. Even the referees for this season-opening Hall of Fame game against the Cardinals were in a labor dispute, leaving a band of confused replacement officials to figure it all out as they went along.

We probably should've hung our heads in defeat and looked to the future for hope. But all over the city, Saints shirts, jackets, jewelry, shoes and hats came out of storage. Wreaths and flags were hung. Manicures and pedicures included a fleur de lis. The city cloaked itself in black and gold. We couldn't know if this season would end in tears or triumph, but we'd be dressed for it either way.

I opened the front door of the French Quarter house as Patrick put out folding chairs. Black-and-gold clad fans spilled out of the bar on the corner and walked past our stoop shouting Who Dats to each other.

The "wailing woman" down the street was locking her door behind her, headed out in a gold corset with black lace trim over black shiny leggings and unreasonably high heels. Her tall, black top hat was decorated with gold lace and a tulle puff at the back. Wherever she was going, I knew she'd return drunk. We all knew. The police had taken to gently guiding her home when she'd wander the street drunkenly sobbing. Taking in the gorgeously appointed home we knew she owned and her always-fabulous wardrobe, it was hard to imagine what would make such a privileged woman so sad. I tried not to let it hurt when she got like that, but it was hard to watch anyone in that much pain.

Patrick was setting up a third chair when I came back inside. I smiled. "Pretty sure we won't need more. Unless you invited someone." He never did.

He arranged the chairs. "I invited Ashley."

"The Traffic Tranny?"

"Yeah."

I laughed. "That's awesome. Is she coming?"

"She's working." He pointed toward the open door. "There goes her whistle. But she said she'd try to get here."

"I only invited a few people and most already had a plan." As he headed into the bedroom, I reminded him, "But I still get credit for the invite. I'm tryin'a make an effort. Otherwise I'm just gonna spend all of my time with you."

Patrick turned in the bedroom doorway and smiled. "Fine by me."

I laughed then heard Wendy's voice behind me. "Hey! It's crazy out there. I had to park in Texas." We met halfway and hugged. "I'm alone. Family emergency. He'd much rather be here, believe me. I brought wine." She held a bottle out and we headed into the kitchen.

Go-cups in hand, we sat on the stoop watching the black-and-gold world go by. A mule-drawn carriage rolled past, it's driver expounding on architecture. We waved. The Saints-jersey-wearing driver and a child on someone's lap waved back. A party bus made it's way up the street. Through the open windows, t-shirted guys sang drunk and loud while other guys danced inside. We didn't wave.

I pointed with my plastic cup. "Bachelor party."

Wendy shook her head. "With that sad, sad 90's rock song?" She laughed. "I thought I'd seen it all and I had NOT seen it all. A bunch of drunk guys rocking out on a party bus to *Torn*?"

The guy in the gold bikini top, black tutu and ratty, black wig strolled past but got no comment. We saw him all the time. Wendy flirted with a dog in a Saints kerchief as it's black-and-gold-wearing walker and I exchanged Who Dats. Mr. Okra, the produce vendor, rolled past in his mobile market – a pickup fitted with bins filled with fresh fruits and vegetables. The city had come together to buy Mr. Okra the truck when The Storm flooded his old one. Dr. Bob had

141

painted nearly every inch of it with local slogans and produce offerings. Mr. Okra held the P.A. handset to his salt-and-pepper whiskers chanting, "I have oranges, I have eating pears, I have mangoes, I have tomatoes, I have garlic..." He was the last vegetable cart vendor in the city. Sometimes I'd spot the mule-drawn Roman Candy cart parked near a park or university Uptown, but Mr. Okra was the last of a tradition of chanting cart vendors. Just like the ice cream man, I usually let him pass without buying anything, but I loved him passing just the same.

I waited for a moment between distractions then looked at Wendy. "I heard Robert's house is still doing stuff. Same kinda things but this is really going on a lot. Either it's supernatural and his house is super active, or whoever's doing this is motivated and tenacious."

Wendy shook her head. "I'm not sure which is scarier."

"I know, right? Can you think of anyone like that? Maybe someone with experience as an electrician or magician or maybe mechanics or special effects?"

She looked at me like I was supposed to know the answer already. "Uh... Emma?"

"Emma? The ex?"

"Yeah, she works special effects. You've worked with her. She was one of the assistants on *7 Sisters*." She waited for it to register. "She helped with all of Brooklyn's explosions. I could swear you met her. We were on that for months. You'd have to have crossed paths at some point."

"Small world. I don't remember her though." I often made this observation. I'd met far too many people over the years.

"Blonde, messy, short hair. Average height. Maybe up to our chins? And she loved overalls. Wore 'em all the time." That seemed familiar. "She"s gotta be ticked all those gutter punks are wearing 'em now."

"Ugh, don't bring them up. I'm so sick of the harassment."

"And the--"

Patrick yelled from the living room. "It's starting!"

I spotted Margie rounding the corner pumping a decorated Who Dat parasol. Wendy must've remembered her from the birthday gathering because she shouted to her. "It's starting!"

I leaned inside the door and checked the giant-screen TV – the commercial was ending. As we piled into the living room, I was reminded how much of the Who Dat Nation was female. Though we had one of the smallest fan bases, every year the Saints were number one in female apparel sales. No wonder the men here wanted to marry.

It was a preseason game of a team hobbled by suspensions and suspicions but from the second Drew Brees threw that first pass, from the moment he led us to our first touchdown of the coming year, we felt nothing but pride.

Ashley arrived sometime in the second quarter wearing high heels, shredded shorts and her Tina Turner wig. She immediately joined in with our cheering and coaching.

After too many inexplicably bad calls from the rookie refs, normally calm and kind Patrick yelled,

"Go back to Foot Locker!" at the black-and-white-striped ref on the screen. I was less kind and clever.

During halftime, we talked about New Orleans hosting the Super Bowl this season. Patrick always knew a lot of stats but we'd all heard this one. "Never, in the history of the NFL has any team won a Super Bowl on their own turf."

Ashley refreshed her vodka-cranberry. "We aim to be the first. Two Dat!"

The Saints were carried to the Super Bowl on a tidal wave of belief and showed us that anything was possible. I Believed. Why not? It was free, it was fun and it had no calories. I liked that Saints fans were believers. We didn't care how it looked to others. And now we were emboldened by having been right once.

All over the city, there were signs that we were prepping to host the Super Bowl. Mostly detour and construction signs. Hotels were remodeling. New businesses were opening. Uniforms were being updated. Cabs got mini-TV's and credit card swipers, and cell towers popped up throughout the Quarter. Maybe we'd finally be able to use our phones during games and parades. The city bustled with the burden and excitement of readying for the biggest game of the year – whether the Saints were playing or not. But it was nice to think all of this inconvenience could be for our own team.

We settled back in for the second half. I loved that the bar down the street always played Angela Bell's *I Believe* after touchdowns. Our TV was on a slight delay from theirs so sometimes we could hear their jubilant crowd erupt just before a touchdown.

Sometimes we could hear a deflated "awww" a millisecond before a dropped pass.

Occasional tourists would peek in our window or through our open door. Margie waved at a tourist in a t-shirt and ball cap. He just stared then walked off. "Odd."

I chuckled. "I know. It's happens whenever we open the shutters or the door. They stand there, noses to the glass, watching us watch TV. It's like, 'here are New Orleanians in their natural habitat. Note the black and gold coloring.'"

Everyone laughed until the next horrifically baseless call made by the refs. The bad calls would have to be the big headline of this game, no matter the outcome. Regularly checking his iPad, Patrick said other games were having trouble as well. This couldn't stand. Life wasn't fair but sports were supposed to be. The heavily-funded, nonprofit NFL just had to take all this randomness and bad judgement out of play before the regular season started. The pro refs' demands seemed entirely reasonable in the face of this kind of mayhem. I needed to believe the madness of this season would stop somewhere.

But I forgot all about it when the Saints won. Watching Drew's first touchdown of the preseason reminded me how much I loved this team and how much they'd done to lift the city. Winning the first game reminded me how good victory could feel when you let yourself care. Maybe we should've been setting our sights lower, but the Saints taught me that truly anything was possible. Besides, my entire career was based on believing odds could be beat. Less than one percent of people in my union made enough money to live, but I'd been doing it for decades.

Ashley left quickly to get back to her corner for the post-game festivities. The rest of us hung out on the stoop as the watching-parties filled the streets and a new kind of mayhem began.

Margie had a gig to get to at some point so we exchanged hugs and Who Dats. Wendy helped us put away the snacks and tidy the kitchen before heading out. Patrick and I fastened the shutters then closed the floor-to-ceiling window and the door.

I gave Patrick a hug and smiled up at him. "Well that was a good day. Ashley was cool. Thanks for inviting her. At some point she went from talking defensive strategy to discussing manicures. Gotta love it."

We cuddled on the couch for a movie and I felt like my life was everything I'd ever said I wanted. The true test of this relationship had been to see if I really wanted what I thought I wanted now that I had it. Though it could be scary to have so much to lose, it was an easy yes.

After Patrick turned in, I jumped onto my computer to work on a blog post about the day. I'd only taken a few photos, mostly of fans in the street. As they were loading, I opened a browser window to IMDb, the International Movie Database, and searched for *7 Sisters*. I still got a kick out of seeing my name in the cast, but I clicked the crew list and searched for Emma. She was listed as "Special Effects Crew (uncredited)."

I clicked her name to see her other credits. There were only five so I started from the bottom, her first job. She'd been a production assistant three years ago on a made-for-TV movie. Next she was a special effects assistant on another TV movie by the same production company. Then came *7 Sisters*. That struck me as quite the step up, and a quick rise as well. Maybe she was really good at her job. Maybe she was well connected. Maybe she was gorgeous. Maybe she was just lucky. Maybe all of the above.

The top two credits were for movies that were still in post-production and wouldn't release until 2013. One had her listed as "Pyrotechnician (uncredited)." The most recent listed her as "Special Effects Assistant (uncredited)."

When it said (uncredited) next to an actor's name, it usually meant that the actor had either been cut from the final product, or that they were a featured background player whose name wouldn't appear in the project's credit scroll. I'd never realized how many of these special effects credits weren't listed in that final scroll. The more I clicked around her projects, the more I saw (uncredited) next to the names of special effects crew. All that death-defying work and they never saw their name crawl up a screen? But I was guessing the pay was good.

I copied her name and Googled it to see if I could find anything else. Emma Brand was a fairly common name. There was even a character on *The Andy Griffith Show* named Emma Watson who was apparently also referred to as Emma Brand in the second and third of her six episodes as Mayberry's town hypochondriac. Barney Fife kept a file on her called "The Emma Watson Case" due to chronic jaywalking. I had to wonder why they'd switched the name for the last three episodes and two subsequent episodes where someone referred to her character. Was there some Emma Brand out there threatening to sue over being seen as a hypochondriac and chronic jaywalker? Emma had been played by Cheerio Meredith. Now that was a name.

I tried adding "New Orleans" to my search. The IMDb page popped but nothing else seemed to relate. I pulled up my Facebook page and tried there. One in the UK. That made sense, it sounded like an English name. Another in Ghana, but it was a man. It was becoming apparent to me how misleading common names could be and why Tate didn't put much stock in them.

I looked up Robert's page and scrolled through his photos. I tried not to feel like I was spying. I always felt a little guilty that my dad's profession had rubbed off on me in ways that could made people more available to me than they realized. But nowadays, everyone looked at each other's information and there was plenty to find without leaving your desk. My only hard rule was I wouldn't pay for information. My guiding principle was treating others as I'd have them treat me. But, I was trying to help Robert, right? It was okay that I was looking through his photos, right? Still, as I scrolled uninvited through personal moments and intimate gatherings, I felt like I was invading his space.

The photos of Emma were down near the bottom, when he'd first joined Facebook. Maybe she'd encouraged him to make the page. The first shot I came to would've been the last one he posted. It was of Emma blowing out candles with money pinned to her chest. Clearly a birthday. The background looked like Robert's parlour. There was a selfie of Emma with Robert standing behind her at a parade. The giant toilet float in the background meant it was Krewe of Tucks rolling St. Charles. I couldn't tell if Robert knew he was in the photo, but he wore no beads which meant he either wasn't trying to catch anything or he put everything in a bag. Either way, he seemed disengaged.

The shot of the couple in tux and gown was both sweet and awkward, like a prom photo. Emma held a mask on a stick. They were probably at a Mardi Gras ball. Wearing overalls, Emma held out a plastic bottle with a coin in it in the next photo. In another, she appeared to levitate a wad of paper between her hands. Magic tricks. So she was capable of sleight of hand and deception as entertainment. And magician and special effects person hit two of my guesses for a suspect.

The last picture that included Emma was of the two of them standing in front of Lafayette Cemetery #1. They weren't touching. Maybe it was a photo from when they both worked that tour. Maybe it was from before they dated. They certainly hadn't been given to public displays of affection either way. It made me feel even more uncomfortable about scrolling through their relationship.

I clicked the message icon at the top of the Facebook page and found a short note from Christine. "Forgot to say – Robert found a puddle when he put the hat back. I resisted joking about Aunt's tears."

A puddle? Like from a leak above the breakfront? It was raining like crazy that day. No, the hat would've been wet on top. Why would there be water after the hat fell but not before? That didn't make sense. And could the water have anything to do with the hat jumping off the breakfront? Maybe it hit a wire and created a spark? Did that make sense?

I looked back to my computer and tried to focus on blogging, but my mind kept working this new puzzle.

Chapter 13

The Red Dress Run was a charitable fun-run that originated in San Diego, attracting 2,000 runners annually. A Washington D.C. chapter was attended by about 600 runners in red. Owing in large part to our city's lack of laws prohibiting drinking in the streets, the New Orleans run hosted about 10,000 people. That said, many of them failed to raise money to get an official number and actually contribute to the charity. They were there to wear something silly and get drunk by brunch. Even so, last year our local chapter raised almost $200,000 and had a blast doing it.

Started by the Hash House Harriers, a "drinking club with a running problem," the original concept revolved around breast cancer but grew to include over sixty non-profits. The story goes, a newcomer came to join the weekly group meeting in San Diego not realizing it was a running club. She arrived in a red dress but, being a sport and dealing with their jokes, she ran the trail anyway. Thereafter, other runners began arriving in red dresses as a joke and, eventually, it became an annual event. I liked the story and it seemed just the sort of thing people here would've done.

Patrick and I headed toward Armstrong Park to take in the ball gowns, sundresses, tutus, silly-frilly frocks and slinky, sequin numbers – some with matching jewelry, hats, angel wings or boas.

The weather was mercifully cool but people came fully prepared, dragging coolers and carrying backpacks full of beer. The many husbands and other men in dresses reminded me of the Buddy D. parade when the Saints made it to the Super Bowl and the streets flooded with men in black and gold dresses. Red-dressed people pushed carts or wagons redone as parade floats (including the Animal House float) featuring loud boom boxes and beer coolers. A busload of stunned people rolled slowly past in an airport shuttle like they were touring a safari. They stared slack-jawed. I often wondered what people made of this place when they had no context for what they were seeing.

The Bucktown All-Stars played a cover of The Meters' *Fire on the Bayou* inside the park. I loved that song. They seemed to be getting a kick out of the ocean of red-dressed dancing drunks. But we'd had enough, so we wound our way toward the Quarter for something to eat. When we passed our place, Dancing Man 504 and Margie were talking on our stoop. Margie smiled. "There you are. We figured you couldn't have gone far but Daryl was just saying he had to move on."

I motioned to the locked door. "Y'all good? You need a bathroom?"

Daryl gave me a sweaty hug. "I'm good. Y'all have a great day." He and Patrick did a hug-pat and he disappeared into the stream of passing people.

Patrick hugged Margie. "We were just going to breakfast."

I smiled. "Yeah, wanna join?"

"I just ate. I'm looking for some of my people. Figured this was as good a place to stop as any since your stoop has an elevated view of the street. Look!" Margie pointed to a group of tourists wandering the sidewalk dragging rolling luggage behind them. "Have you heard of this thing, AirBnB?"

Patrick hung his head and shook it. "I keep seeing those people. Always big groups too. They crash in someone's house like it's a hotel. Except the homeowners don't have to pay the fees and taxes hotels do, or pay employees or install sprinklers or fire escapes and they don't have to price in the market. Some guy was renting his back yard as some sorta campground experience."

Margie put her hands up like she could stop what he was saying. "I saw that. He said it was a glamping thing but there's no toilet. He gives you a bucket and access to the hose."

I wasn't sure I understood what they were talking about. "Is it like timeshare?"

Patrick motioned to the group working on a lock box across the street. "The owner gives you a code to get the key."

"And you just live in their house? Like with their stuff in it? Strangers just use your stuff? I don't get it. Wait, so how am I supposed to know if someone is breaking into their house or if they're supposed to be there?"

Margie sighed. "You don't. And you don't have your neighbor there if you need anything. My friend lives next to one and there's always loud parties with horrible music and they leave trash all over the street.

She's been cursed at and two guys exposed themselves to her."

New Orleans had all the assets and troubles of a major metropolis but it was actually a pretty small city with a population of under 400,000. But because tourism was the city's major economy, on any given day New Orleans was filled with at least a million people. Far more during our more popular seasons. It meant walking behind people staring at maps on their phones or moseying and window-shopping on the same crowded sidewalks we used to get to things on time. Same with driving – gawkers and lost people blocking the flow of daily commuting. It meant supping next to tables of people in t-shirts who didn't know to leave the dining area to talk on their phones. It meant being patient with two-thirds of the people you might encounter in a day.

I loved meeting the people who came to see a culture they'd fallen in love with from afar – the music and food lovers, and people who were into our architecture or history. I liked giving them directions, fun factoids or recommendations. Very few of us had patience for the people who came only to drink on Bourbon, pee or vomit on the street and leave. It seemed odd and paltry to base a trip on that as a plan. And it felt insulting that anyone would say they'd been here and not bother to see anything locals were a part of other than as employees. It'd be like going to Brazil, never leaving your hotel grounds and thinking you'd experienced the country. The idea that locals were making it cheaper and easier for strangers to find places to stay here scared me. "Shouldn't you have to stay in the house with the people to make sure nothing bad happens? What if they just take all your furniture while you're gone? And why are we encouraging people with no money to come here? Shouldn't we be promoting this place to people in the mood to spend? Now you can just rent someone's yard and walk around with a six-pack?"

Patrick nodded. "Yep."

"Well that makes no sense. It's bad enough we've given up on Bourbon, which used to be this swanky street of supper clubs, dancing halls and burlesque theatres. Now that we've turned it into a red-light district with Big Ass Beers and t-shirt shops, now they want to encourage broke people to stay awhile? The stay-cation crowd wasn't poor enough? No wonder we can't fix anything. We're actively courting the lowest earning vacationers. Patrick's always sayin' we should charge a toll for tourists to get into the Quarter since so many people drive in from Kenner and wherever and don't always get rooms for the night. And won't this jerk money out of the hotel's pockets? And that's our tax money, so maybe Patrick's right."

We stood silently for a while as the run started and thousands of people ambled past. The front rows jogged while everyone else milled and meandered. Margie spotted some of her friends and waved. I recognized a few of them from the friends I'd met through the only other guy I'd dated in the city, Tom. He was how I'd originally met Margie. Tom was a fan of my blog but warned me to be careful who I shared this place with – saying that it was our duty to protect New Orleans and keep it special. I imagined he hated this BnB thing. Margie hugged us and pushed through the crowd to join the waving friends as we headed to a side street.

The line at the Camellia Grill wasn't bad and we got two stools in Ricky's section without having to let people in front of us. With Pepto-Bismol pink walls, and crisply-uniformed waiters, the place was like a southern-fried set from *Twin Peaks*, wacky and wonderful. Ricky took our orders and yelled them out to the line cooks. Then he chatted us up while polishing every piece of silverware before gently placing it, untouched by human hands, on our napkins. He took the same untouched-by-human-hands care in offering me a straw. The waiter in the other island of seats sang to his customers and offered each fist-bumps as they exited. I showed Ricky my ring and he called the guys over to congratulate us. I loved how happy love made people here. Anything was a good excuse to celebrate but love topped the list above any accomplishment or holiday. One waiter made me a rose out of a paper napkin and they all congratulated Patrick on a being a lucky man.

Patrick cut into his chili cheese omelet. "I have a pair of green shorts and I'm tryin' to think of a costume for Mardi Gras. I bought 'em on Amazon and they're shiny like wrestler shorts."

"But you don't want to be a wrestler?"

"Maybe the Green Giant?"

I smiled. "What about a super hero?"

"I could be Green Goblin."

I nodded while finishing my mouthful of grits. "But he's a bad guy."

"I could be the Incredible Hulk. He's kind of a good guy."

I laughed. "He's a moron, an aggressive moron. He just gets mad, growls and breaks things."

"I could go as Green Lantern. I could go as a superhero who was a box office disappointment."

I laughed and nudged him. "You're terrible."

Ricky brought us a piece of grill-heated pecan pie and a chocolate shake with two straws. "On the house."

I hoped we'd have the kind of wedding where we could include people like Ricky. I wanted to be able to invite people we only knew one small way but who were rooting for us as a couple. It seemed smart to strengthen our support system in that way, by knitting together the big and small pieces of our lives for that one day.

On the way home, we stopped at Matassa's Market so we wouldn't have to go foraging for food later. The family store opened in 1924 and featured a couple aisles of groceries, a deli and a short-order cook. I was happy to see the legendary Cosimo Matassa sitting behind the register, ready to bag our groceries. In L.A., New York and D.C., I'd grown used to people who had accomplished fairly little but promoted themselves like they'd invented cool. The elderly man tapping the keys of the register and arranging items in bags had just been inducted into the Rock and Roll Hall of Fame. The studio owner, producer and recording engineer responsible for hits by Fats Domino, Ray Charles, Little Richard, Dr. John, Ernie K-Doe, Jerry Lee Lewis, Sam Cooke, Aaron Neville and many more, Matassa was credited with helping to develop the rock and R&B sounds of the 50's and 60's.

It was funny what could become normal. In L.A., it became normal to stand behind Michael J. Fox in line at the bank or sit next to Laura Dern in the chiropractor's waiting room. Here, it was normal for people you knew to have a Grammy or to have played at the White House. I loved that the legend who helped create the soundtrack of my parent's lives was also the man who'd been a staple at this store for three generations.

After a lifetime of leaping into unknown places surrounded by unknown faces, it felt good to be surrounded by such rooted people as I explored my own roots here. Born away from the rest of our family, I grew up feeling like I was far from home. We didn't eat what our neighbors ate and our manners seemed strange to some. Maybe that's why I found the courage to quit my jobs, sell my house and make the move to New York to study acting. I'd visited the metropolis plenty as a child and made the three hour trek once in a while when I got a car. I knew my way around a little, but everything about it was foreign and not-home, just like my birthplace. I knew I could never really live in New York so once I finished school and started getting work offers, I left before the money could seduce me.

I'd been to California but only San Francisco. Los Angeles was just images in movies, TV shows and magazine photos for me – and I knew almost nothing about it. I knew zero people there and arrived with no address. Richard Dreyfuss had recommended an acting teacher when I stayed to talk to him after seeing him perform on Broadway. All I needed was a job to pay for the classes. I sometimes marveled that I had the courage to make that leap. People would tell me I was brave, but I was so busy figuring out how to accomplish everything that I never gave myself time to be scared. I didn't feel brave, I felt busy.

The leap to New Orleans was different. I had family here, memories and favorite places. I moved into a house that's smell reminded me of childhood.

When we got back to the French Quarter place, there were half a dozen people having a party on our stoop. They jumped up to let us in, then picked up their wagon's handle and moved on.

I emptied groceries into the fridge. "Do you know anything about the guy who owns that tour company everyone works for at some point? Lou something?"

Patrick was silent. I still had to remind myself that didn't always mean he hadn't heard me or was ignoring me. Sometimes it meant he was working on the problem. I waited to see which time this was.

Patrick yelled from the living room. "Lou Salvaggio?"

"Does he own a tour company?"

"The one with all the Garden District tours. And those haunted ones. Do you know this guy? Buncha lawsuits."

I joined him on the couch as he scrolled articles. "What kind of law suits?"

"This one's some guy suing for workman's comp."

I laughed. "As a tour guide? He got tendonitis in his pointer finger?"

"No, it's something about compensation. I misread it. I think he was suing for wrongful termination. Yeah. He wanted a severance package I guess. Jules Mouton. Doesn't say if he won but I could probably find out."

"Yeah, but what were the other ones? You said there were a bunch of law suits."

He clicked around. "This one is for breach of oral contract." He read for a while. "Okay, so she's suing because they had an oral contract that she would develop her own tour. She said he promised it would be her tour and she'd get a percentage no matter who gave the tour." He looked up at me. "So, it's like she's copywriting the tour." Back to the screen. "But he says no agreement existed and that he owns all routes and tours exclusively. Anything she came up with while hosting his tours is automatically his property."

"It's like one of those contracts the restaurants make the chefs sign that says the restaurant owns any recipes the chef comes up with while working their menu. Wait, no. It's like the opposite of that."

He smiled. "Only there was no contract. She just trusted him."

"Or she made it up."

Patrick chuckled. "Cynical. But yeah, could be."

"Did she win?"

He scrolled. "Doesn't say. Hold on, I'll look it up. Emma Brand."

"Wait, what? Did you say Emma Brand? That's Robert's ex."

"Yeah? She didn't win but it looks like it dragged on a while so it probably cost Lou a lot."

I nodded. "That could really irritate a person. It would make me crazy."

"She said she had emails. That was the point of it all I guess, these emails backing up the oral contract."

"That seems solid. Why didn't she win?"

"She never produced them. She said they got erased."

My face pinched. "Erased? From the server? She never copied them to her desktop or printed them?"

"It just says she delayed and delayed then finally said they were erased."

"So she was either telling the truth and we have no idea what happened, or she was lying and tried to carry the lie on forever like she wouldn't eventually get caught. What is that? Entitlement? Compulsive lying? A break from reality? Immaturity? The inability to grasp consequences?"

Patrick looked up from the screen. "Maybe she just wanted to teach him a lesson. Expensive lesson though."

"Right? And time-consuming. It would require malice over time – intensity, tenacity and malevolence. Kinda like what's going on over at Robert's house."

He scrolled some more. "Robert is listed as a character witness."

"For which?"

"For Emma."

I took that in for a moment. "Which could be another reason for Lou to hold a good, long grudge for Robert."

Patrick nodded. "Plenty of bad blood to go around."

Chapter 14

Reuben's table read was out in the country. I slowed to spot the gate hidden somewhere in bayou brambles. I pulled to the intercom and pressed the button, waiting for someone to buzz me in. Though the surroundings were decidedly different, waiting to be let onto gated property seemed like old times.

There was a house near the top of the road, then a big, beautiful lake on the left. Ahead on the right was a lush swamp and past that, a larger, grander house. I rolled past it to the parking area behind. There was a baseball diamond with a catcher's cage and bleachers, a pavilion full of picnic tables, an enclosed industrial kitchen and dining hall, a giant barn with a theater marquis out front and a gargantuan hangar-type building on the other side of a massive field of grass. In the distance was a neighborhood-sized pool. And that was just what I could see from my spot next to the charging station for the owner's electric car. Where was I?

People were gathered near the fire pit in the back of the house so I headed there instead of trying to figure out which door to approach. I immediately recognized John Schneider talking to Reuben. Ah, the gate did say JSS. John Schneider Studios? John Schneider Sanctuary?

Though his smile glowed, John didn't seem to

recognize me as Reuben introduced, "This is Charlotte that I was telling you about from *7 Sisters*. She'll be playing your wife."

And just like that, we were married. "Hi. We've met actually. But I'm just now realizing I was wearing a pink wig and burlesque costume." Reuben's face went sideways and I laughed. "I was parading with the Pussyfooters, you know, the pink ladies from the Mardi Gras parades."

Reuben nodded. "Yeah. Yeah, okay."

John extended his hand and smiled again. "So that's who was under there. Yes, I was with the guide and he knew your friends."

I smiled back. "Exactly. This is your place? You live here? In Louisiana?"

"Planting roots." He motioned to the land. "Yeah, it's a little over sixty acres. Used to be a church camp."

I nodded slowly. "Ah, I get it. That's why the pool and baseball and dining hall."

"There's a river too and a bamboo forest."

"These are sets? You shoot here?"

He looked genuinely proud and happy, something I wasn't used to in celebrities. "That's the idea."

"Are we shooting here? I mean, it looks like you could shoot a dozen movies here without using the same set twice."

Reuben stepped in. "We're figuring all that out. Show her the inside of the house. There's a screening room and edit bay. In fact, why don't we all head in and get started."

It wasn't a question. I followed them through the sunny kitchen, past rows of chairs in the screening room, through the living room full of antiques, and into a large dining room to a long, aged table full of water bottles and scripts. Though he'd been on TV since 1979, I was embarrassed to admit I'd never seen John's work before. I wasn't sure if Reuben had chosen John because of the studio facilities or if John was one of our producers, but as we read through the story, he seemed a good fit for my husband. Over the last couple years I'd seen a few husband choices come and go, but I hoped this one stuck.

It was my first time meeting the other actors, though I recognized a few of the faces as locals who worked a lot. Everyone seemed fairly easygoing, something I always looked for at a reading. Any actor asking a lot of questions about the script set off alarm bells for me. But I only really feared the ones who asked for dialogue changes this early in the process and in front of everyone. It usually meant they would be entirely focused on their own performance, not the movie writ-large and the demands of production. They were likely to be the ones who got insistent with wardrobe, hair and makeup about the look of their character long after the director had signed off on decisions. They were apt to improvise without warning, maybe grabbing their fellow actor or trying to "keep it fresh" in some other potentially upsetting way. And they were prone to hating their lines, demanding rewrites and changing words on camera against the director's wishes. It may've been an honor to work with some of those people, but it was never easy.

I drove back to the city feeling fairly certain that my patience with this project coming together was finally going to pay off. I was excited to call Claudia and tell her about the progress but decided to wait until after my visit with Robert. He offered me a cool drink as I settled into the couch in the sitting room. Robert poured us two teas from a pitcher in the kitchen and held out an icy glass. "Sugar? It's not sweet tea."

"I'm good, thanks. Christine said you found a puddle on top of the breakfront?"

He stopped short of sitting and crossed to the cabinet. "Yeah, up here." He circled his finger above the cabinet.

"How big a puddle?"

He came back and sat across from me. "Not big. A few ounces."

I got up from the couch and took in the antique breakfront with handblown glass panes. I pointed at a nearby chair. "Do you mind?"

"Here." He retrieved a stepladder from the entryway cupboard and set it up for me.

I'd probably pointed at some zillion-dollar Chippendale or something in my ignorance. I looked down at the wooden top of the breakfront and lifted the edge of the top hat. "You dusted?"

Robert nodded. "When I cleaned up the water."

"Show me with your hands how wide the puddle was?"

He lifted his hands and made a diameter about the size of a saucer.

I looked back to the hat. "And it was where the hat had been?"

"Exactly. It hadn't been dusted for a while so I could see exactly where the hat had been."

"And was it like a circle or had it been splashed around?"

"It was messy toward the back."

I looked behind the cabinet but it was too dark to see anything. "Do you have a flashlight?"

Robert rummaged in the kitchen and returned with a pen light. It didn't provide much light but I could see there was something hanging from the wall. Could it be a Voodoo talisman? I climbed down from the ladder and shot the light between the antique mahogany and the hand-painted wallpaper. A nail stuck out from the wall holding a mousetrap on a string. A small lead weight hung from the back of the trap. "Did you hang a mousetrap back here?" I moved to let him see.

He peered at the contraption. "No. Why would anyone?"

"Does it mean anything in Voodoo or Hoodoo? Hanging a mousetrap? Is that a thing?"

Robert shook his long hair. "Never heard of that. And I like to consider myself a bit of an expert. I don't get it."

"Can I move this away from the wall a little?"

We shoved the heavy furniture forward a bit and I slid my hand in to pull the mousetrap toward the top. "Hold this." I climbed the ladder again and Robert handed me the mousetrap. I pulled it to the top of the cabinet and it stopped short of where the hat sat. "So if this were pushed against the wall, the trap would sit around the back of the hat." I looked at the mousetrap and the hat, then moved the hat closer to the trap, finally sitting it on the edge where the snap-bar would be if the trap were cocked. "I think I got it."

166

"What it means?"

"No, how the hat flew across the room. What if I put a big piece of ice here where the cheese goes and I set the hat on the bar? When the ice melts, the trap snaps and sends the hat flying. But they have to make sure the trap doesn't go flying so they attach a weight then nail the trap to the wall behind the cabinet. The trap springs, the hat flies, the weight pulls the trap backward and the nail stops it from falling on the ground below the cabinet. That's it. That's how they did it."

He looked at me with a mixed expression. "So there's definitely a living person doing all of this."

My feelings were mixed as well. "I would say you have a ghost-free haunting happening here."

Robert held his hand out to help me down. We left everything as it was and sat. He took a sip of his tea and pushed his hair back from his shoulder. "I don't know whether to be impressed with their ingenuity or terrified that someone came up with all that and was in my home in an effort to scare me and make me second guess my own mind."

"Can you think who might feel that way toward you? Who might be that determined and industrious?"

"Lou from the tours has no love for me. But I wouldn't have given him this kind of credit. And I know Christine has never liked Emma, but we left things on good terms I thought. Especially considering she ended up dating a friend of mine."

I cringed. "Oh, ouch."

He took another sip and wiped his well-groomed moustache with the back of his hand. "Yeah, when I left Lou, mad as I was, I didn't want to leave him in a lurch. So, I recommended this friend as a replacement. Then he commences dating my girl minutes after we break up."

"Guess he took that replacement thing too seriously. What an ungrateful jerk."

Robert's eyes went wide as he nodded rapidly. "That's not even the worst of it. He ends up getting fired and suing Lou which Lou blamed entirely on me. And honestly, I get it. But like I said, Lou's more the slash-your-tires kinda guy when it comes to getting even."

"Wait, your friend sued Lou for wrongful termination? Was his name Jules something?"

Robert looked nervous. "Jules Mouton, yeah. Why do you know that?"

"Patrick looked Lou up and found the lawsuit. But didn't Emma sue him too?" It seemed clear Robert couldn't see Emma as being the same as his jerk friend.

"Yeah and Lou holds that against me too because I served as a character witness for her."

"I can see how that could hurt. Do you think it's possible Emma and Jules influenced each other's lawsuits?" I knew if I asked if he thought Emma encouraged Jules to sue, he would shut down. But I did need him to see things as they were. "I think she filed hers first. It definitely lasted longest."

Robert was quiet. Then, "She could drag things out. She had the stamina for that sorta nonsense."

"And she knew the story of the marbles, right? She coulda been the one who mailed them with the note. She knows where your family's buried? It's just something to think about. Maybe it's not malicious. Maybe it's about money. Maybe she's developing a tour of her own just like she wanted. Maybe she's just goosing the story to promote it. I'm just sayin' we don't really know why someone would do this, but maybe it's just as simple as – 'cause she can. She could've had a key made so she doesn't even have to break in. She probably knows a lot about your schedule and habits. Makes more sense than Lou creeping around looking for an open window."

"What about Jules? He's the kinda guy who takes advantage."

"That's an excellent point. But frankly, it seems like you already gave him all you had to give, and he's not the one who sued over having his own tour. It's just something to think about. Try seeing the whole thing from Christine's perspective. She's someone you trust, she knows everyone involved, but she's not involved. That's a much more reliable perspective on the situation. Just try it. Maybe you'll remember something."

"Wait!" Robert popped up and left the room for a moment. He returned with the Mason jar of marbles and handed it to me.

"These are the infamous marbles? These are cool. I coulda never left them to the whims of the world." I turned the jar in my hands, the marbles clinking on the glass. "Seem harmless enough."

"You know what I remembered the other day? When I was about four, I started hanging out with your cousin, Luke."

I gasped and smiled. "Seriously? That's before I even knew him. He was seven when I was born."

"He was a year older than me but we got along pretty well as kids. He liked my marbles."

I pictured my handsome older cousin as a small child playing marbles with a younger Robert. Luke had passed long ago but I still had such strong memories of him. I felt suddenly connected with Robert. He knew my family. He'd been inside our home.

Robert chuckled. "Sassy's pralines. I lived for Sassy's pralines."

I laughed. "We all did. So you knew Sassy too?" He knew people Patrick had never met.

"After my parents passed, I fantasized about her being my mother."

"Yeah, she was the other mother to so many of us."

"What a woman. Spun from molasses. She used to tell us this uncomplicated version of the *Iliad*. It was just the parts about Cassandra, Paris, Hecuba and Eunoe."

I felt suddenly envious picturing Luke and Robert sitting at Sassy's knee as she spun some version of the passed-down story. "Her family names. Do you remember it? The story?"

"Sure. Vaguely. She started with Eunoe being the daughter of the river god. She has Hecuba who marries the king of Troy and is queen during the Trojan War. Hecuba has Paris and Cassandra – Sassy always left Hector out of her version. She'd tell stories of Paris' heroism and how he married Helen of Troy if we had time, but she focused on Cassandra, the prophetess. The sad story of her rejecting Apollo's advances and being cursed to always know what would happen but never be believed in her warnings. People thought her insane. That part particularly bothered Sassy. She always ended with Cassandra going to the glorious Elysian Fields upon her death because God could see her clearly. That's how she said it. God could see her clearly and judged her worthy."

I wiped an errant tear. "Wow. We did, you know. We took her second line down Elysian Fields when she passed."

"I know. I was there."

I laughed and cried a little at the same time. "I feel like I should hug you."

Before I could rise, he put his hand out. "I think I might owe you an apology."

I couldn't imagine what harm he could've done me that required an apology.

He clasped his hands. "I think I'm the source for the chandelier story on the tours. I know I am. Another guide and I were walking past your house years ago and I mentioned playing there as a kid. He said he'd heard the house was haunted and I told him about the horse buried in the yard and the long journey with the chandelier. But I never said it was haunted."

"It's fine. Seriously, don't worry about it. You didn't even do it on purpose."

"Well, it's been bothering me, especially with you being Luke's little cousin. So I called a woman I know in Cloutierville and asked her if she could help you out with finding your family farm up there."

"Wells Plantation? Seriously? Does she know where it is? Does it still exist? Can I see it?"

He chuckled. "I'm gonna let the two of you speak and stay out of it. I figured you can choose what you care to share with me now that you know I was ground zero for your house being on the haunted tours."

I laughed. "Dude, I came here after eighteen years in L.A. I have a blackbelt in gettin' over betrayal, and yours doesn't even register as a mild annoyance."

He laughed. "Okay." He nodded slowly and smiled. "Okay. So, this is her number and she's expecting your call."

We did finally hug when I left. We both heard the loud thump-thump-scratch from somewhere above. I smiled and pointed at the ceiling. "Mechanical rats. You should go up there and check it out. Find a better flashlight and poke around a little. And think about what we talked about. See if you remember anything new. You never know what you might find if you open your mind a little." I knew he liked to believe he was free thinking so I hoped it motivated him.

The walk home felt a bit magical as I imagined being little Robert walking to play with Luke. I pictured him bursting through the gate and running up to the front door carrying the Mason jar of marbles. Sassy would open the door. My chest filled with love remembering her generous smile and the tickle of her tight afro on my cheek when we hugged. I remembered the house as it was before the renovations. Young Luke came running in from the backyard and yelled, "Come on." I pictured them playing marbles then sitting lotus-like, staring up at Sassy as she rewrote Homer's *Iliad*. Wait. Homer. Homer Wells. Daddy Wells, owner of the Wells

Plantation and all the slaves toiling there. Owner of Lottie, mother of Eunoe, Sassy's grandmother. Whoa.

So Sassy's family names came from their owner being named Homer. Either those names were chosen for them by the owner, or Lottie chose them to leave a trail back to where the family had originated. That made more sense. Lottie was born a slave and Eunoe was as well, but Hecuba was born free and still passed the *Iliad* names. And Sassy named her children Violet Chiffon and Azure Taffeta to lead them back to their birth mother if they got curious some day. The family was big into leaving breadcrumbs. I was excited to tell Taffy and Chiffon that their family had left a trail back to Wells Plantation. It made me feel like maybe I was supposed to tell them and I hadn't broken some long chain of secrets. But then what was the secret I was supposed to be protecting? It seemed strange the family hadn't passed the actual secret to Taffy and Chiffon. Maybe Sassy hadn't known it either and couldn't have told them what she didn't know. Maybe that's what their family thought was best. But it seemed odd.

I left a message for the woman Robert had spoken to in Cloutierville, Catherine Garrett, then starting setting up our new home studio. Patrick had gotten me a super-compactible set of lights and backdrops for my birthday. More and more frequently, my auditions were done at home with Patrick filming and reading lines with me. I hung the white backdrop over the assembled metal frame then assembled a filtered light box and a bulb with an umbrella diffuser. I was setting up the tripod for the camera when Patrick came home. "Hi baby, I'm almost ready for the audition. Do you want to do it now or after supper?"

"Let's just do it." He kissed me and put his bags on the ground before picking up the script I'd highlighted for his lines.

"Let's just read it."

We went through the three scenes then focused on the first one and began recording. Patrick liked the third take and we moved on to the next scene, then the next. I marveled at Patrick's ability to rise to the occasion of me. He'd worked all day fighting to keep our city safe from corporate greed and destruction and wasn't even fed before working at my job.

I knew it wasn't always easy to be my partner in life, especially for someone who wanted nothing to do with showbiz. I tried never to take any of it for granted. Then I opened a can of Blue Runners, chopped an onion and got to work on some red beans and rice.

Chapter 15

Though I'd never been, we weren't planning to attend the Mid-Season Mardi Gras festivities. Living in New Orleans was a series of choices. Should we go to the Sunday second line or catch a favorite band and food booth yummies at whatever festival was happening? Should we go to the Uptown parades or hit Barkus, the dog parade in the French Quarter? But when the Saints were in the Superdome, that's where we wanted to be. Even if it was still preseason.

I had to admit I'd started getting excited for Carnival about three weeks ago, so Mid-Season Mardi Gras seemed well-timed. It was almost ingenious that football season was starting and would carry us through right up to Mardi Gras and the Super Bowl we were hosting. Just at the moment when it felt like it'd been too long since our city was celebrating, the Saints returned and carried us back to Mardi Gras.

We'd been looking forward to seeing the new *Rebirth* statue capturing the moment Gleason blocked the Falcons' punt in the first home game after The Storm. On Sept. 25, 2006, the Saints returned to the rebuilt Superdome. Saints fans were used to losing and most fans didn't know much about Sean Payton or his find, Drew Brees. There was a concert featuring U2, Greenday, Trombone Shorty, New Birth and Rebirth Brass Bands. After that, no one expected much other than to be entertained by their lovable losers.

On the fourth play of the game, Saints' Safety Steve Gleason, in a spectacular move, broke through and blocked a punt and Cornerback Curtis DeLoatch ran the ball into the Falcons' end zone. From every account I'd ever heard, it was the loudest moment in the Dome's infamously deafening history. The crowd went bananas as they realized something new was happening. The moment turned the tides to a 24-3 victory and began an amazing season of rebirth for the team, the Dome, the fans and the region.

Because life was not fair, Gleason was diagnosed with A.L.S., Lou Gehrig's disease. But he continued to inspire. Not only was he an amazing human being with an enviable attitude, he was also a new dad and the founder of Team Gleason, a foundation striving to help those with A.L.S. and their families. Gleason and his blocked punt became the symbol of that moment when hope was born anew. It was the perfect choice for the new *Rebirth* statue. I waited my turn then posed in front of the monument as Patrick took a few photos for the blog.

Patrick had been on the wait-list for season tickets for years but it was easier to get Willy Wonka's golden ticket to the Chocolate Factory. There could be advantages to hopping around the Dome. It would've been great to know our seat neighbors but it was also fun jumping in and crashing their parties. This time, the people we met were also new to the section. The guys sitting next to us were brothers, a twelve-year-old attending his first game and another, much older, who was waxing nostalgic about sitting in the same section as a kid. He hadn't been to a game in years and was excited to finally get to *Stand Up and Get Crunk* in the Dome, though he assured us he did it in his living room after every touchdown.

Going to a Saints game was like attending church. There were rituals, times you stood or sat, singalongs, dances and lots of praying for Saints. But it was also a lot of work. We were silent when Drew instructed his huddle, but when the team was on defense we took our role as the "twelfth man" seriously. We screamed, stomped, clapped and made as much racket as our bodies could generate so the opposing team couldn't hear each other when calling the play. I'd say it was just a fun way to keep fans engaged, but I'd seen it work several times. It felt way more interactive than voting for a singer on your phone. It felt like the closest I would come to being an actual Saint.

The way-more-affordable preseason tickets meant that a lot of the people in the crowd didn't know the rituals the season ticket holders kept going. The crowd only really got loud on third downs. And the substitute referees were truly beginning to wear on our nerves. We commiserated with our frustrated neighbors and hoped the league straightened things all out before it mattered.

The best moment was when the Saints, down by two touchdowns, scored and we all danced and got Crunk. Before I properly settled back into my seat, our boys got the ball back and made another touchdown! I danced like no one was watching, like I was filled with the spirit. Then, somewhere in the midst of all of that, I saw a woman on the Jumbotron and noticed she was wearing the same shirt I was wearing. Thomas Morstead kicked the ball and the screen went black before I realized, "Hey, that was me!"

Patrick looked up then back to the field. "I missed it."

I'd been privileged enough to have appeared on big screens all over the world for years, but I honestly never even dreamed that I would appear on the big screen in the Dome. My phone vibrated in my back pocket. A text from Wendy. She'd spotted me on the Jumbotron. I was happy I had a witness. And I loved what a small town our city could be.

The Saints beat the Texans 34-27 and we all spilled out onto Poydras, taking over the wide boulevard. Kids banged on upturned paint buckets, guys sold beers and water out of coolers and a brass band played *When the Saints Go Marching In*. We passed tailgating parties with meats grilling and music playing, then walked Bourbon toward the house. Black-and-gold revelers wandered in and out of bars chanting Who Dats. For locals who mostly avoided the place, Bourbon Street was best on game day. Fewer tourists and everyone in a good mood.

The phone vibrated in my pocket as wind chimes sounded. I didn't recognize the number but the place was listed as Cloutierville, Louisiana. Patrick closed the door behind us and twisted the deadbolt as I gave him a small smile. "I have to take this. It's the Wells Plantation lady."

He headed to the bathroom and I answered. "Miss

Catherine?"

"Yes. Charlotte?"

I smiled. "Yes."

"Robert tells me you're kin to the Wells family."

My heart sped. "Yes."

"I wasn't able to find much but I'm sorry to tell you the house burned to ash sometime in the early 1900's."

I felt my heart fall to my stomach.

"I couldn't find anything about the cause of the fire. I have an address for you but I rode past there earlier today and I'm not sure you'd find it worth the trip."

"Oh?"

She sighed. "It's very cheerful, it's just not my taste."

I loved how gifted southerners were at turning a criticism into something lovely-sounding.

"I knocked on the door but the new owners didn't know much about the place's history. So I looked in the census and found the home was last listed as belonging to a Creole family. Darlin', I'm sorry to say that doesn't tell us much because this area became known for its Creole settlers. There's no record of the property changin' hands after that until the new owners purchased the place from the bank in the late 80's."

"Do you know the family's names?"

"Yes, hold on." She rustled some papers. "Leonard Bird Wells, wife Daisy, daughter Birdie."

I felt a chill. "Daisy and her family took over the farm? But they weren't a Creole family. My family is almost entirely English-American all the way back to the early1600's when we were just English."

"Not according to the census. It lists Leonard and Birdie as Creole."

"How strange that no one ever told us we were part Creole. That's my father's grandparents and mother. You'd think someone woulda mentioned it."

She took a breath. "You young people are freer in your thinkin'. It was different times."

I always found that answer paltry, but she was being exceedingly helpful so I let it be.

"City records listed the farm as belonging to Miss Daisy Wells. Robert must've gotten it wrong, he told me the place belonged to your mother's side."

I chuckled. "It did. Daisy was my maternal-great-great-grandmother's sister. It was different times, I guess."

She tapped her papers on a table. "Mister Leonard apparently passed in the fire but as I stated earlier, I couldn't find any articles or records of what set the blaze."

"So Daisy was a homeless widow with a daughter?"

"There's no further record of the mother and daughter in Cloutierville, or of where they could've gone. The sheriff tried to get some items they'd found on the property to Daisy and Birdie but couldn't find any trace of them in Louisiana. It was stuff they found when they dug the new foundation. An old Bible, a china doll, things like that. I think the sheriff ended up sellin' them."

"What a shame. I would've liked to see those things, stuff that belonged to my family."

Catherine sighed again. "I can imagine. I'm sorry I'm not able to do more. We're not much of a place compared to New Orleans, but do let me know if you decide to venture this way. I'll be happy to escort you around."

That's very generous of you, Miss Catherine. And thank you for all the digging you did. I really appreciate it. My family will too."

We said our goodbyes and I stared at the wrought iron fireplace grill in front of me. Miss Catherine had given me answers but now I had so many more questions. Was I part Creole? Why hadn't anyone mentioned it? How did Daisy end up back at the farm? Since it now seemed clear Leonard Bird Wells also got his name from the family plantation, was he a cousin? Was he a slave? Was that what they meant by Creole? Were they hiding his heritage after the war? I knew if I were in the Garden District house, the chandelier would've been jumping off its chain.

I opened my laptop and searched the Cloutierville address on Google Maps. The Wells Plantation land had been subdivided and peppered with suburban houses. I dropped the little, golden, virtual man down onto the address and the street view popped onto the screen. I spun the vantage until I found the house and immediately understood what Catherine had meant by "cheerful, it's just not my taste." The house was banana yellow with the pillars, shutters and trim done in a paler yellow, like the inside of a banana. I appreciated the effort they'd made to use local architecture styles but the whole vibe was more wannabe replica than refined homage. The land was fenced so I wouldn't feel comfortable wandering the property without permission. Maybe the owners would let me in, but they didn't know anything about the land's history and it all just looked like yards now. I felt comfortable not making the journey. Everything seemed erased.

Patrick peeked at my screen. "Wow. Yellow."

I laughed. "They really went for it, right?"

"Whose house is that?"

"It's the house the new owners built where Wells Plantation used to be."

Patrick gave me an empathetic smile. "I'm sorry. I know you were hoping to see the house." He kissed me. "I'm gonna find us something for supper. Do you want Dreamy Weenies or Moon Wok?"

"Either's good." The food was tasty but we really loved the families that ran the places. I kissed Patrick again and locked the door behind him. Then I rang Sofia and waited.

She answered breathless and laughing. "I thought I locked my purse in the car but Nia said the keys were in my hand."

"You're out and about?"

"We're at ballet class so I have some time. Nia's so cute. You would die. She hardly ever does what the class is doing. She's got this whole interpretive dance thing going. She gets all carried away. It's adorable but I think the teacher isn't a fan."

"Heck with her if she can't take a joke. It's supposed to be fun, right? Nia's six."

"I think the teacher's hoping to find the next..." Sofia started laughing. "I just realized the only ballet name I know is Baryshnikov."

"Rudolf Nureyev, but that's another dude."

Sofia laughed. "Alvin Ailey."

"Jeeze, why don't we know women's names?"

"I know, and I think of ballet as a woman thing."

I laughed. "Me too. But remember in L.A. I kinda made that rule that I wouldn't memorize women's names until the third time I met them? Seems so gross now, but it was just common sense there."

"It's not your fault. The guys were always the same gang but the women rotated all the time. There were a few girls we saw more often but they were the ones the guys all seemed to get around to at some point. And they were the ones who were willing to share. Remember when a bunch of them went to Vegas with two of the guys. It was like six women. Not to be mean, but I'm not sure the guys knew all their names. And they spent a weekend with them."

I gasped. "Remember that time that agent asked me to find out the name of the girl he was at the Malibu house with? She was in the jacuzzi and he asked me to find out her name and tell him."

"And they'd already spent the night together. So you're not that bad."

"Still, I don't like that I participated in the dehumanizing."

Sofia laughed. "We called Tom 'green gloves guy' for weeks. Even after you were dating. You're an equal opportunity dehumanizer."

I laughed too. "That's terrible. Seriously, we're awful."

She started cry-laughing. "You called your ass your costar."

"I did. Oh man. That's really awful. And I thought it sounded so cool, like I was really owning my power."

She calmed herself a little. "You were. Women don't have a lot of language for ego stuff."

"When I held those auditions for that short film I directed, we saw over a hundred women. I was the writer/director. I was paying for the whole thing out of my pocket and I'd written every part for women. But when they came in to audition, well over half of the women looked and spoke to my producer, the only man in the room. I left wondering how many times I'd done that at auditions. We're supposed to be the culture leaders in my business and we're so far behind on equality."

Sofia chuckled. "What do you expect from a place that's basically the Playboy Mansion? When my mother came here from Italy, she was shocked to see the women competing for men. She said it was unnatural."

"Seriously? My southern belle mom called it an unnatural imbalance of power. They both said unnatural. That's kinda heavy. But I did find the guys out there unnaturally lazy at seducing women."

Sofia laughed. "That's because, 'wanna see my boat?' works on a lot of girls out here."

I laughed too. "I'm so glad I don't live there anymore. And I knew I'd never find Patrick out there. He would never live in a place like that."

She got serious. "But it was so worth it, all those pitiful dates with rude, horny guys were worth it because it got you to Patrick. You got really good at being alone but you could only go so high doing everything alone. Without a tether, a kite is just torn paper in a tree. You need that anchor to let you fly high. And now you're in the biggest moment of your career so far and you don't even live here. Think about that. You're getting ready to dance in Mardi Gras parades. Your life is so fun now. I saw how bad it all sucked. I listened to every painful detail. And I know it's easy for me to say, but I feel like it was worth all of it."

I laughed. "You always said that I'd feel that way when I found the guy, that I wouldn't care what it took. But honestly, it was nothing if Patrick and this life was what it was leading to. Dating had its moments. I met some of the most amazing men in the world. Most just weren't very good relationship material. Or dating. Or just plain good company. But some were fascinating. And I coulda only really had access to them there. And some it was actually amazing. I mean, I do get that I'm partly complaining about dating movie stars and billionaires." We both laughed. "Yeah, it was worth it if this is what it was all leadin' to. Thank you for always sayin' that even though I got sorta combative toward the end." I mocked myself, "All evidence to the contrary! You've been sayin' that for over a decade!"

Sofia laughed then snorted. I could barely understand her for the cry-laughing. "At what point are you going to question your conclusion?"

My sides were hurting. "Oh no, I said it so many times, you memorized it. Oh man, I'm so sorry."

We both cry-laughed for awhile, unable to speak. It was such a great release of all that we'd been through over my battered heart. I was so blessed Sofia moved to L.A. She brought out the school girl in me just when the town was beginning to take a toll. I slowed my breathing. "Thanks. Seriously, I don't know how I could've stayed okay without you there. And I know it wasn't always fun for you so thank you for that, for reminding me to believe, for all of it. If I was there, I'd hug you."

"Some of it was fun though. I got to dance to *Satisfaction* with Mick Jagger because of your dating life. I went to a bunch of premieres because guys wanted you there without a guy. I hung out at mansions, being served poolside in Malibu. Mostly because you were single. Mostly because nothing ever worked with any of those guys, so you were available but you hadn't really been with anyone in the group. They liked us. They loved having you around. Yeah, sucked for you that none of them claimed you or made you feel like you'd found someplace safe to land, but we got to do a lot of fun things just because they liked us. Since I was totally focused on Mark, for me it was all just fun. I got to hang out with Jack Nicholson at the very first party you took me to, remember?"

I laughed. "Okay, then I'm not sorry. Heck, you owe me." I calmed. "We're even. The whole thing is even. And I came out way ahead."

Patrick opened the door carrying bags from Dreamy Weenies. I hoped he got me the spicy dog with the grits on the bottom and the chili cheese on top.

"I gotta go. Patrick's got these amazing hot dogs. I don't even like hot dogs but these are delicious. Okay, gotta go. Thanks again."

I smiled at Patrick them kissed him. "Welcome home."

Chapter 16

Hurricane Isaac was scheduled to make landfall on the seventh anniversary of Katrina hitting the Gulf's shores. It was hard not to freak out a bit. We decided to stay. The storm was much weaker and the levees had been rebuilt (though we had no reason to trust they'd been built stronger than the ones that failed since they were built by the same people). I closed and latched the shutters, then tied them together with shoelaces.

Driving through the neighborhood, many of the long door and window shutters were latched shut. The stylishly painted accents usually gave the elegant homes a touch of whimsy or style. Now they looked ominous, like eyes closed shut against impending danger. Especially the windows boarded with plywood.

Like everyone else in the city, we headed to the Walmart to stock up. We ran into Tina from *7 Sisters*. She was picking up party provisions to ride out the storm with friends. Lots of people were out and about, all with one question, "You stayin' or goin'?" It seemed about 60-40 staying, much lower than in the pre-Katrina days for a storm this size. People were clearly spooked.

The water aisle was already empty. Jumbo packs were being sold straight off the pallets. The beer and wine aisle was picked over with entire shelves sitting empty. Ramen noodles, canned goods and chips were flying off the shelves. The cart traffic was pretty chaotic. There was only one flavor of CLIF Bars left and no nine-volt batteries. But, the checkouts moved swiftly and our cashier said she would be working the next day. No one was panicking, just preparing for the probable power loss and a few days without stores. Plenty of people had under twenty items – though the recent college arrivals were buying cartsful and enough water to bathe for weeks.

While we put away all the groceries and supplies, my brother Tate called. Patrick motioned that he was going to take a shower then whispered, "In case we have to go without water for awhile."

Dang, I should've thought of that, especially with the premiere of *7 Sisters* coming in a few days. If worse came to worst, I could pull my hair into a chignon and throw on a Dr. Boogie hairpiece.

Tate clicked keys on his computer. "Hey, you got a minute?"

"I'm so glad you called. The lady from Cloutierville called. The Wells Plantation burned down in the early 1900's and now the land is a neighborhood and the place where the house stood is this banana-yellow house that wants to be a plantation when it grows up."

Tate chuckled. "That sounds awful."

"I'll send you the address and a screenshot. You think I'm exaggerating the yellowness of it, but you'll see. So, she didn't know what started the fire but it killed Leonard Bird Wells. Oh, 'cause he, Daisy and Birdie were the last people to live there. Daisy Wells,

Lily's sister. Birdie, Dad's mom. So weird. You realize that means that farm was the birthplace of both sides of our family at some point. And there might be more relationships. Like who is Leonard Bird Wells to the rest of the family? Was he related to Daisy?"

"That's why I'm calling. I've been looking into that area, Cloutierville and the Cane River region. Cloutierville is a registered Creole Colony. It was founded in 1822 so nearby plantations and lumber companies could have access to supplies and services. That could explain why so many different things have the Wells brand on them, but don't forget that also means those items could've belonged to anyone."

"Except the chandelier has Lily and Daisy's initials on it and Dad got that pipe from his grandfather, who turns out to have died in that house. But, you could be right about the flask. No tellin' who it came from."

He kept clicking on his computer. "So the Cane River region is known for its Creole culture. In particular, there were generations of families living side-by-side, owners and their children next to slaves and their free children. So sometimes when they say Creole, they don't mean part-French or Spanish or whatever, they just mean mixed."

"Sure. Wait, before you go on, I have to interrupt. I forgot to say the biggest part. We're part Creole, did you know that? Why wouldn't anyone tell us we were part Creole?"

Tate stopped clicking. "Wait. Why are you saying that?"

"It was on a census. Leonard Bird and Birdie were listed as Creole."

Tate chuckled. "I was calling to ask if you'd thought about Leonard Bird being born a slave."

"Yeah, but he could just as easily be a cousin. I'm not sure how we can find out which one is our story."

Down the hall, I heard rattling. "Ha!" I knew that story would get the chandelier going. "I'll be right back." I dropped the phone, grabbed my camera and ran down the hall. I pressed the power button and slid to a stop in the bedroom doorway. The chandelier was undulating. The crystals looked like the tiers of a a stadium doing The Wave. The camera clicked and clicked. Then the crystals dropped and settled into place just as Patrick came in from the shower.

Wrapped in a towel, he slid past me. "What're you doing?"

I gave him the one-minute finger and ran down the hall to the phone. "You still there?"

"Yeah, hey, I gotta go."

My phone beeped. "That's my other line. Talk soon. Bye." I saw Clarence's name and clicked over. "Hey! Are you here?"

"No. I'm not calling with great news."

Please don't say I'm cut. Please don't say I'm cut. "What's going on?"

His voice was gentle. "Are you safe there? You're staying?"

"Yeah. We should be fine. Even if we lose power here, we can always go to the French Quarter place when the storm winds down. The Quarter almost never goes without power."

Clarence seemed sad somehow. "Charlotte, I'm

not coming. None of us are."

"For the premiere?"

"Yeah. I'm so sorry. I was really looking forward to it. I loved the local crew there. It was like a no-panic zone. And I wasn't easy on 'em. Long days."

I was trying not to cry. "They'll be so disappointed y'all aren't coming. Dang, seriously?"

"Yeah. I'm sorry."

That didn't help. "Will there still be a premiere?"

"They're calling it a screening. No red carpet."

A tear escaped and I felt a little silly crying over not getting to wear a pretty dress. "No red carpet?"

"In case things don't look so great down there, I think they just want to avoid the whole story."

"Wow." I felt less sad and more angry. "That's really... it's so fear-based. Man, that place runs on fear. Jeeze. All these people did all this work. And I know I'm not the only one that got a fancy dress."

Clarence sighed. "You should wear it anyway. Don't you guys like to dress up for no reason there? Just wear it. Send me a photo."

I chuckled. "Okay." Patrick came into the room. "Thanks for calling me. I appreciate you being the one to tell me."

"Yeah, of course. I'm so sorry Charlotte. I really wanted you to have this moment."

That did help. "I know. Thank you for all of it. I can already tell this one's gonna be great. I can't wait to see it." I hung up, checked to make sure the phone was off then dissolved into tears.

Patrick held me. "What's going on? Is everyone okay?"

I laughed. "That put it all in perspective. Yes,

everyone's fine. They cancelled the premiere."

"For 7 *Sisters*? Why? Isaac? I told you I was worried about that."

"I know but I figured it was too expensive to cancel that much free advertising. I guess they figured no one ever went to a Clarence Pool movie 'cause of what someone wore on the red carpet."

"That's probably true. He's got a heavily male, geek-leaning audience." He held me to his chest again. "I'm sorry, baby. Are they still gonna show us the movie at least?"

"Yeah. Clarence told me to wear my dress anyway and send him a photo."

Patrick smiled. "I think that's a great idea. And you know I won't miss the red carpet."

I chuckled. "I just feel horrible for Lisa, the designer. This happened to her before. She supplied clothes to a movie and got cut. She was so excited. This was gonna be her big break to make up for not gettin' that break." Then the tears flowed.

"Aw, I'm sorry. I know this was gonna be huge for you. You worked so hard and you were finally gonna get your turn to shine."

It was hard not to feel a little sorry for myself. "They still figure out new ways to hurt me."

Patrick lifted my chin. "Let's go for a walk, get out and clear our heads. You can tell me all about it if you want."

It was likely we wouldn't be leaving the house again for days. "You're right, let me grab some shoes. But I'm done with the pity party. Only privileged people get to cry over cancelled premieres."

The sky was that foreboding green that often

192

arrives before a storm. The weather afterward would likely be gorgeous. I snapped a couple photos of boarded windows and panes crisscrossed with tape. Carried by wind, my hair kept flying across the lens.

Robert texted, "I found something" and we headed for his house.

Patrick opened the gate. "Spooky trees. Must be dark inside. Keeps it cool, I guess."

"All of the above – spooky, dark and cool. Oh, plan on having a cool drink."

Robert swung the tall door open and invited us in from the wind gusts. "Can I get y'all a cool drink?"

Patrick smiled at me. "Sure, what d'ya got?"

"Iced tea. Lemonade. Water."

We made our selections and Patrick followed me into the sitting room. I showed him the breakfront I'd told him about and the hat sitting on top.

Robert handed out icy glasses. "I'm so glad y'all were out. I really wanted to tell you about some of the things I found. Once I knew to look in cracks and search for contraptions, I found quite a few things. I'm truly certain you don't want to go into the attic, but there were timers setting off those thumps and scratches we heard. She'd rigged a spring-loaded weight and pulley system attached to boots on golf clubs. They would fall, thump, thump, then drag back across the floor before resetting. That was the scratching sound."

"Huh, I found a spring near your gate once. But you said 'she.' Have you figured something out?"

Robert pushed his hair back. "I tried to see things clearly, to not be blinded. I tried to see it through Christine's eyes, like you said." He nodded toward me. "Christine's only motive has always been friendship. I figured it might not be a bad idea to see Emma through her eyes and ask why she felt so protective of me when it came to Emma."

I smiled. I loved that acting techniques had given me so many inroads to the way people worked. It made compassion and empathy easier and blame harder, but it could be eye-opening. Cathartic even. "That's good. That's really smart. And what did you see?"

"I remembered Emma talking about her tour idea. She said she deserved her own tour and that I was a sucker for giving all of my best stories to Lou for free."

Patrick and I both said "oh" at the same time.

"Yeah. Then I remembered a time she got jealous thinking I was running around. She sprayed my headboard with her perfume. Saturated it so it smelled for days on end. If she had a key, she could've done that with my aunt's talcum powder and my dad's cologne. Not on the headboard, on the walls and-- she could've let herself in and saturated stuff."

Patrick interjected. "Marked her territory."

I resisted bringing home the dog reference. "Wow. And she knows how to rig special effects. And she can be persistent with a grudge. And she wanted you to believe in hauntings. And the house being haunted might help her with some tour she's cooking up for herself."

Robert looked at his hands. "Sounds like a lot."

"It is a lot. So are you going to confront her?"

He looked startled. "I don't know for sure that it's her."

Patrick chuckled. "You sound like Charlotte. Gotta be extra-special certain before you confront someone. Confronting someone could help clarify if they were involved."

I smiled at Robert. "I've been learning the value of taking the vagueness out of things. Besides, if it is Emma, remember she also knows pyrotechnics. Do you really want to be so polite that you risk pyrotechnics with someone who had access to your key?"

He nodded slowly then looked to us. "You have to understand that it's a difficult for me to see her as a villain."

I got that. "But can you see her as single-minded? Or maybe self-centered? Territorial? Can you see her choosing her own thing over you? I mean, didn't she? A few times?"

He looked down to his hands again. "Yeah, I can see that."

Patrick picked his tea up from the gold-trimmed crystal coaster. "You're already not together, what's the worst that can happen? I wouldn't be able to sleep at night wondering what she might do next."

I laughed. "Yes you would." I smiled at Robert. "He naps at Mardi Gras parades. Seriously, sits in a folding chair behind everyone catching beads and just sleeps. Brass bands, sirens, giant speaker systems, the whole nine. Unperturbed."

Robert was laughing. "Sounds like a superpower to me. Kudos monsieur." He tipped a hat that wasn't there.

"Practice makes perfect." Patrick stood and stretched. "We should get going. Do you need help with anything before we take off?"

Robert stood. "I'm good. Doesn't look like much of a storm. I think we'll all be fine. But thanks." They shook hands and Robert led us toward the door. "Oh look." Robert opened the cupboard and pulled out a mechanical rig. "From the attic. I had to take it apart a little to get it down from there but you can still kinda see how it worked. There were weights attached to the back here. And these wires went to the pulleys."

"Wow. Elaborate. And the pulleys were screwed into the ceiling?"

"The rafters, yes."

"Whose boots and golf clubs?"

Robert cocked his head. "Mine. I thought that was weird."

"Yeah, but missing boots and golf clubs would just seem like more haunting, right?"

Robert chuckled. "I guess so."

I hugged him and headed back out under the green sky. Once the gate was closed behind us, I semi-whispered. "She didn't bring boots and golf clubs 'cause she knew he had them. Who else woulda brought all that rigging and not bring the boots and golf clubs unless they knew for sure there would be some here? Also, you'd have to know when Robert was leavin' the house and for how long 'cause that had to be time-consuming to rig all that and I'm guessing it was noisy. But like, she could've even used his own tools. One less thing to carry past nosy neighbors. It had to be Emma, right? No one else could've done all of this in this way. Even the ice cube, mouse trap thing only really works if you can set it up, get out of the house and know Robert will be home before it melts. Or maybe she stayed in the house. Ew, and was there when we were there. In any case, the whole illusion works best if he's actually home when it happens, right? And who would know all that? Emma the special effects specialist ex-girlfriend, right?"

Patrick laughed. "You're the only one who feels the need to check and recheck. You don't exactly jump to conclusions."

I followed Patrick off the sidewalk toward a new restaurant, Mia's Balcony. "Are we eating? I didn't dress."

Patrick laughed more. "I doubt anyone's gonna care. Look." He pulled the door open and the cozy, contemporary place was entirely empty.

A host came out from the kitchen and greeted us. "Hey, feel free to sit where you like." We took the table in the window and settled onto stools as the host handed us menus. "We're serving a special Shrimp and Crawfish Corn Bisque today. Let me know if you have any questions."

The menu read like a list of my favorite foods. I hoped it tasted as good as it sounded.

Patrick took my hand and smiled. "Get anything you want. This is our last supper before the rain hits but it's also our Charlotte-deserves-a-fuss dinner."

Life's unnecessary roughness was so much harder to weather before Patrick. Without him, I'd be at home eating something from a frozen box feeling like I wasn't worth cooking for and sad to eat alone. I'd be scared of the storm coming, unsure if I was equipped to handle days of wind and rain tearing at the house, losing power and sitting in the dark with no TV. And I'd end up focusing on how disappointing it was to have our premiere cancelled when this storm would be long gone by Friday.

Instead, I was laughing and in love. I was the only table being served in a new restaurant with a view of streetcars gliding tracks on St. Charles. I was eating a grilled tomato with slightly melted mozzarella plated beautifully with basil, balsamic glaze and roasted garlic cloves.

Our host turned out to also be our waiter. It had to be impossible to get employees to travel with this weather coming. Though it was a little spooky sitting alone in the restaurant, bathed in the green light of the ominous sky watching debris gust past, it was also kind of romantic. Certainly a little funny. At some point, we wondered if maybe our host/waiter had also cooked our meal. Maybe he was the owner and didn't normally do any of these jobs. He probably should've just closed but we were glad he didn't know that.

I had a bite of Patrick's delicious filet mignon with chimichurri sauce, asparagus and roasted potatoes before devouring a perfectly ripe avocado stuffed with crabmeat and drizzled with balsamic glaze.

There was a short lull in the wind as we walked St. Charles and headed back to the house. Lots of people were out walking their dogs during the break in the blustering. Some just let their dogs out in the yard, waiting on their porches and staring out at the strange sky.

Chapter 17

The rain was hammering the house, pelting it with sheets of water. It was far too loud and scary to ignore. A leak ran down one wall and I put a towel on the floor to sop it. A tornado warning beeped loudly on Patrick's cellphone. We pretended to focus on a game of Scrabble after the power went out but I jumped a few times reacting to thunderclaps. Then we heard what sounded like the rumbling of a train. We knew it could be a tornado so we ran into the hallway and waited for the rattling windows and trees branches smacking the house to pass.

In all the fuss over the premiere and the storm arriving, I'd forgotten to show Patrick the photos of the chandelier. Before we settled back into pretending to play Scrabble, I grabbed the camera and looked for the first shot.

Patrick put his hand up. "Please don't take a picture."

"I'm not. I wanted to show you something." I held the camera in front of him. "Here, scroll through."

He took the camera and pushed the forward arrow. He stared at the picture, then pushed the back arrow. He clicked back and forth between the two a couple times then kept scrolling. He went through all of the photos then handed the camera back to me. "There's so much electricity in the air right now, I'm shocked the whole house isn't bouncing."

"I took 'em yesterday while you were in the shower. Seems like you would've felt something like that if you were showering in electric air."

He placed tiles on the board and counted his super-high score. Twice. I waited for some sort of reaction. He grabbed the bag and pulled six tiles, placing them on his wooden holder. "Your turn."

I waited for him to finish arranging his tiles and finally look at me. There were very few times our age gap showed up but I'd learned long ago that though men of all ages sometimes needed time to gather themselves, younger men could really press the point. "What do you think of the pictures?"

He looked to the board. "They're strange."

"Yeah. Yes. Even stranger if I'd taken a video. But it was all happening too fast. I got what I got, but you have to admit that chandelier is moving on it's own. I'm not crazy. Look! It's right there. A thousand words, right there." I pointed to the little screen on the back of the camera.

"I saw. It's definitely weird."

I chuckled and shook my head. "It moves on it's own. I'm just sayin'." It was clear that his logical brain was having a very hard time facing something so illogical. I got that. I liked when things made sense. But I also liked when things felt miraculous. Even though it could scramble my brain, I liked when life became magical, when coincidence crossed over into fate. I was willing to admit that I might not understand how the world worked, that it might even be unknowable. That was harder for Patrick. He liked certainty. I was glad he had Job-like patience for my kooky career. I couldn't even be counted on to deliver a premiere for a movie I'd worked on for months, the most anticipated movie I'd ever been involved with, a movie where my character was included in the title. I knew I had to tell Lisa Iacono but I was trying to avoid using my computer battery and there was no wifi anyway. The home phone was dead without electricity and it felt gross to text the news to her. So I waited. And I carried the anxiety of wanting that moment behind me.

It was a little like camping when Patrick and I ate supper. We had a gas stove so I was able to cook up some pasta with a zucchini and tomato sauce. I was careful not to open the fridge more than necessary, but I checked my plastic containers and they were still frozen solid. I'd prepared a lot of things in advance like freezing a bunch of containers full of water and using them to keep everything cold in the freezer after the power went out.

I'd filled the cast iron tub with water in case we had a boil advisory or lost access to water and needed some even to flush the toilet. I'd stocked up on canned goods and dry goods. I'd done all the laundry, charged all the electronics and unplugged anything that wasn't surge-protected. I'd dusted all the decorative candles and made sure there were plenty of plain pillars for backup in a drawer. Patrick checked the batteries in the flashlights, took out all of the trash and lined the door to the back porch with tape and a towel.

But nothing prepares you for the relentlessness of sitting in a darkened house in the daytime as the elements test the limits of walls, windows and the roof. I would've said that only an actor could remain calm amidst that much chaos, but Patrick was doing a great job of normalizing things as much as possible. I suppose it was mercy that just surviving the storm safely was a good distraction from thinking about the premiere. It was hard not to dwell on yet another moment ripped from me right when I could've gone to the next level. I'd survived it plenty of times before but I'd believed Clarence when he said I'd finally get to shine. He said he'd written the part so people could finally see what I was capable of – and that could still happen. I was missing out on branding, networking and exposure. But I was still going to be seen by a generation of movie lovers and filmmakers.

But there was another thing that tugged at my brain. Even if it was a common name, why were there two Leonards that came from same place? Were they related? Patrick took a short nap on the couch and I shuffled through the piles on my desk looking for the family trees I'd printed. I sat on the floor and placed them side by side. Lily Wells married Leonard Oliver Perry, the overseer, and they had Oliver. I looked to the other tree. Leonard Bird Wells married Daisy Wells and they had Birdie.

Birdie hated her name because it was like her dad's name, so it might be safe to assume Leonard Bird Wells went by Bird. Bird Wells. Since it wasn't an uncommon custom, Bird could also be his mother's maiden name. Same with Leonard Oliver Perry. His mother might've been an Oliver.

I looked through the tree to see if I found any other Olivers or Birds, something else to connect the two Leonards. Leonard Oliver Perry had also been the one to sign the bill of sale for Lottie on behalf of the Wells Plantation, the one Bryan Batt bought for his shop at an estate sale.

There didn't seem to be any other connections so I checked everything again looking for ties between Bird Wells and Lily and Daisy Wells. Other than his marriage to Daisy, I couldn't find any connection to the family. It seemed so strange that they would all have the same last name. And Bird had the same first name as Lily's husband. It felt like a sudoku puzzle with too many numbers missing, just enough exposed to be frustrating.

My cell rang and I grabbed it before it could wake Patrick. Tate. "Hey."

"I've been calling for an hour. Couldn't get through. You doing okay? It looks really bad on the TV. They keep showing old photos from Katrina. I hate when they go for those emotional buttons like that. Just tell us the news. If I want drama, I'll watch a soap opera."

I chuckled. "We're okay. It's scary and we don't have power but we're fine. Patrick's napping."

Tate laughed. "Okay. I'm gonna stop worrying so much."

I knew him too well. "Try at least."

"Since you're fine, the Cane River has been heavily documented. There've been studies, historical registers, books, all sorts of stuff. I found that census and that lady was right. It lists Leonard and Birdie as Creole."

"I'm pretty sure he went by Bird. Remember the names were supposed to be similar?"

"Okay, so I kept looking and I found a census

from the 1860's. It lists the occupants as Homer Wells, wife Iris, and their four kids. No Creoles."

I thought about it. "That makes sense. If Bird was a cousin, he probably wouldn't have lived there. And if he was a slave, he wouldn't be listed as an occupant of the house."

"Right, so I started looking for slave listings. I found a site that had a bunch of them online. I didn't see anything for the Wells Plantation so I emailed them."

I felt excitement rising. "Did they write back?"

"Yep. And they sent me a copy of an inventory of assets from 1860. I emailed it to you."

"We don't have wifi."

He clicked his computer keyboard. "It lists first names, ages and value."

"Gross."

"They would probably all go by Wells for a last name. Okay, it says 'Bird, infant.'"

My heart jumped. "Bird? Is that when he was born? Daisy was born around then so yeah, that makes sense. Oh my gosh. That's it? We found him? You found him."

"Yeah."

"And he was a slave."

"Yeah. No idea if he was mixed or if the Creole thing was just a cover for after the war, but that's him."

I was beginning to understand a possible reason why no one told us we were Creole.

"I wrote them back and asked if they had any record of Birdie since she was listed as Creole. They'd followed some of the families as they spread across the country so I thought it was worth a shot. They said to search obituaries for Birdie's name."

"Why? We know where she passed. Oh! 'Cause if she was listed as next of kin, it might tell us where Daisy moved to."

"Yes. And I found them in Texas. So I got a library there to look through their census records and they found one that listed Daisy and Birdie."

"Oh my gosh! Tate, you're amazing at this."

"Here's the thing. Birdie isn't listed as Creole."

I thought about that for a minute. "So, the house burns down and kills Daisy's former-slave husband. She moves to Texas, but not the same area she lived when she and Lily ran away with Leonard Perry and Eunoe. So Daisy probably doesn't know anyone there and more importantly, they don't know her. It's an opportunity for a fresh start. In Texas. Where there's no such thing as Creole culture. And Birdie had that curly red hair and freckles like she was from Ireland or a Viking or something. Maybe it was just easier to hide her heritage than to try the Creole thing in Texas. Her dad could've been anybody they said he was. Wow. Do you think Birdie knew?"

"It depends how old she was when the fire happened."

"Catherine just said the early 1900's. Birdie would've been a toddler at most. Who knows if she she knew, but it might explain why she called her parents trash. And why she didn't like havin' a name like his. Oh, I don't like this. Did she know and not tell us 'cause she was ashamed or something?"

Tate took a pause. "There are the things we can know and the things we'll probably never know."

"I'm tryin' to think why Sassy's family always had to hang the chandelier. I'm fairly certain it was to hide the secret they supposedly protected. But I'm pretty sure the initials carved in the top were L.W. and D.W. for Lily and Daisy Wells. So why hide that?"

"Maybe they were afraid people would think they stole it. Back in the day, lots of people got arrested on rumors if they weren't from the right neighborhood."

I chuckled a little. "Back in what day? Yesterday? But Lily or anyone in our family would be able to explain to the law that we'd gifted it to their family so it doesn't seem like enough of a motive." I heard the chandelier rattling in the bedroom. "Why wouldn't Sassy's family want anyone to see the initials and the symbol?"

"Maybe Eunoe was reported as a runaway and that would identify which plantation she'd come from."

"Yeah, but hadn't the war ended? And she was traveling with people from the farm who could say the report was mistaken, that Eunoe was still working for the family, not a runaway. Again, seems like she was kinda protected from the worst of the worst happening if that's what she feared."

Tate clicked at his computer again. "It's a head scratcher."

I thought he might be looking something up, but enough time went by that I figured he was probably just trying to multitask. I attempted to engage him again. "I think it's wild that Mom and Dad's families married twice."

He laughed. "That we know of."

206

"And we're descended of slaveowners and a former slave."

"That's not as weird. It's more odd that we're finding out about it."

I chuckled. "Yeah, I guess."

The chandelier was really shaking now. I looked to Patrick sleeping on the couch and decided it wasn't worth it to try to wake him. By the time he came to, the activity would probably be over anyway.

Tate clicked some more. "I gotta go. And you need to save your phone."

"Oh no, I wasn't even thinking. I got carried away by the story. I mean, Daisy and Bird married like a hundred years before the Civil Rights Act granted them the right to marry. And Lily ran away with the overseer. It's all pretty wild. These were women willing to take a leap. The men too."

He was still clicking, still not interacting. He wasn't great at multitasking.

"Okay, wish us luck."

The chandelier stopped rattling, settling into a rhythmic tinkling sound.

Tate's clicking stopped. "Be careful, okay? I'll try to call you again after Isaac passes."

I didn't bother checking on the chandelier but I did wonder what new trick it might have pulled. Why did it have to hang? What secret were Eunoe, Mama Heck and Sassy protecting? Why didn't Taffy and Chiffon know the secret? Each new answer revealed how many questions were still were left to resolve.

Chapter 18

To our north, south, east and west, there was devastation. But for the most part, New Orleans was spared. Still, hundreds of thousands were without power and it could take weeks to get everyone back on the grid. Ditto for wifi, cable and landlines.

After the major community events of shopping for supplies and preparing for the oncoming winds and rain, the storm itself was a fairly isolating experience. So when we finally took to the streets, it was wonderful seeing people. Swapping stories, we caught up with other rattled-but-grateful neighbors.

Trees were down and debris was everywhere as we drove to the French Quarter – the best place to find electricity and food. Despite the storm, another party was getting started with scantily clad dancing and drinking men arriving daily for Southern Decadence. We were just glad to have access to food and a working TV to watch the Saints game.

The French Quarter stood as an oasis of services in a region still fleeing flood waters. We went searching for a meal as tasty as the one we started the hurricane with during our private dining experience at Mia's Balcony. Walking around, it was easy to spot the tourists, all boozy and optimistic, in the crowd of locals wearing house-dresses and galoshes on their unscheduled "Hurrications."

We found the newly opened SoBou, owned by the same culinary geniuses behind Commander's Palace, and decided to give it a try. Due to the storm, we were told the menu was limited but I was happy from the second I was offered a cold glass of water from a pitcher filled with fruit and ice while Trombone Shorty played on the stereo. The dining rooms were decorated with hundreds of glass bottles and a few of the tables featured beer taps. A gauge measured pours and priced them accordingly.

But we were there to eat something that didn't involve a can. The Pork Cracklins went for only a dollar so that was a must-try. We shared a spicy Three Melon Gazpacho with shrimp and Cochon de Lait Gumbo served with potato salad. But the big treat was the little SoBou Burger – a griddled patty, bruléed onions, pepper jack cheese, pickled okra mayo, and cayenne ketchup served on a brioche bun.

We made our way back to the house through the thickening crowd of drag queens and scantily clad male revelers. Wendy was just pulling up as we arrived. "Hey!" I was glad for the timing since text messages could take a couple hours to arrive and cell service was terrible.

I kissed Patrick goodbye and jumped into Wendy's car to return uptown. It was probably crazy to go back through the downed power lines, branches smashed onto the roads, broken traffic lights, and upturned portalettes. But it was only about three miles. Determined to pamper ourselves, we parked in front of a bar with boarded windows spray-painted with "BAR OPEN, FOOD, FOOD," and crossed to the spa for our massages.

The front room of Belladonna's was a clean-smelling retail collection of shower shoes, luxurious lotions and relaxation-related gifts. We shopped while we waited and I caught Wendy up on the Robert situation. She wasn't as surprised as I thought she'd be to hear I suspected Emma.

Though I felt anxious and self-indulgent walking in, Lakietha was able to coax a lot of the tension from my body. It'd been a long time since I'd given myself a true day of pampering to prepare for a carpet. I wasn't going to let the cancellation rain on my personal parade. Both my mother and Patrick had said I deserved to celebrate my accomplishments so I tried to focus on their voices and not the overwrought racket in my head. I'd definitely had too many days of forced camping, so I was struggling with focusing on the negative – even as the biggest moment in my career was unfolding.

Wendy looked glowy and refreshed. I hoped I looked like that too. She threw a bag of candles in the back seat then pulled her car onto the first one-way to turn around. I gasped. She slammed the brakes instinctively and we both snapped against our seat belts. Wendy looked around, then at me. "What?"

Lowered in my seat, I pointed toward the windshield. "It's Emma."

Wendy pulled off the road and sunk into her seat. "She knows me!"

My eyes followed Emma in the sideview mirror "Where is she going?"

Wendy peeked out the window. "Isn't Robert's house a block from here? Maybe she parked away from his house and is heading there."

In the rearview, I saw Emma open a car door, grab a bag from the passenger seat and shut the door again. Her alarm chirped.

"Stay low."

Emma walked past and we watched her disappear around a corner. I realized I'd been holding my breath. "Do you think she's going to his house?"

Wendy sat upright. "Should we follow her?"

I found my phone and texted Robert, "Are you at your house?" It seemed like a long time before he texted back, "On tour. Talk later." I looked at Wendy. "Do I tell him we think she's heading there?"

Wendy pulled a phone from her purse. "If you don't, I will."

I texted again. "Check your house when you get back. Saw Emma in the area." I looked up at Wendy. "Send, right? Is it too accusatory?"

"She could be at his house right now."

I pressed send. "It's his thing now. He gets to figure out whether he wants to press charges or hug-it-out or whatever."

Patrick was still doing something on his iPad as I started my transformation into a glam girl. Even if he'd starred in the movie, men never had to go through what women did to make a moment happen on the red carpet. Reporters asked the guys about their role and preparation. They asked us about our designers and what it was like to work with the men. The whole approach put undue pressure on the desire to make some fashion splash or show more skin than the others dared.

I played makeup artist and stylist, pulling

together my Lisa Iacono dress with black jewelry and strappy, studded warrior-princess stilettos. Standing in front of the full-length mirror, I was sad the look wouldn't get its moment, that Lisa wouldn't get the boost she was hoping for and that I, once again, was having to remember the difference between being humbled and being humiliated.

I wasn't sure why this pattern repeated, me getting right to the precipice and falling short of the next big leap. But I had to admit I'd made many choices along the way that slowed my roll at least as much. I'd never had a taste for fame but I would've liked to have had more choices, more access to better roles. The days of competing for leads in movies like *Jerry Maguire* and *Lord of the Rings* were behind me, and back in Los Angeles. I had no plans to return to L.A. after *7 Sisters* even though I knew it would put me back on radar and give me a great shot at a starring role during pilot season. I'd almost always chosen my peace of mind over money or fame. Though this was a big bounce in my career and any sane actor would've exploited the moment, I was finally happy with my life.

Three photographers stood on the sidewalk in front of the Prytania. One of them was shooting photos with their phone. Patrick smiled. "Look, a red carpet."

I laughed. "You must really love me 'cause I know you're horrified to see any photographers."

Patrick got us popcorn while I posed. It was wonderful seeing so many familiar faces as we looked for a good seat. Tulip, my makeup artist, was draped in a caftan with butterflies scattered throughout a leafy-looking fabric. It was the first time I'd seen Tina without her signature Saints hat with the ponytail pulled through the back. I almost didn't recognize her with straightened layers framing her face instead of a cap pulled over her eyes.

Everyone was so nice and seemed genuinely happy to see me. Patrick leaned into my ear. "You know you're the only sister here. You're the biggest star in the room."

I hadn't thought about that. I looked around at the actors, stunt people, painters, drivers and all the other local people who'd contributed to the movie and realized I hadn't allowed for any upside to the premiere being cancelled. We were about to have an entirely local experience of this globally anticipated film. This might actually be fun.

It's customary to clap after the names of every producer, the lead actors and the director. At most premieres, we clapped after every opening credit, louder if the person is in the room, louder still if they were the star. Clarence wasn't with us but his name caused an eruption in our theatre. We were all grateful for our jobs and the experience. The stars got little applause since they weren't there. It was jarring for me to see a name like megastar Graham Paisley flash across the screen and have almost no one bother to clap. But he'd only been on set for a week or so, and we'd all worked together for months.

My name was on the first "shared card," the term for more than one actor's name appearing on the screen at the same time. It was one of the many terms I'd had to learn during contract negotiations over the years. My name was with Aliyah Thomas, the last of the *7 Sisters* listed and the woman who'd truly had my back on the project. I felt real-life sisterhood with her and was really sorry our paths weren't crossing again. Then I heard the clapping and whistling and people yelling my name and realized the calamity was for me. Patrick was right. For tonight, I was a big fish in a small pond. And it felt kinda nice.

I tried not to be disappointed when the funeral scene was accompanied by The Isley Brothers' *That Lady*, though it had originally been my character's song for her entrance into the pool hall. It could be difficult to really experience the movie at a premiere. So much of my brain could get occupied by the movie that wasn't there – the scenes and actors that had been cut, the unexpected changes in tone or plot. There were also fun laugh-moments we never saw coming, but I often needed to see something I was in at least once again to experience the movie the paying audience attended. It was also dangerous to trust the cast and crew to see our work with a critical eye. We'd invested ourselves in the scenes that played out.

Early in my career, I'd been standing in video village with a director, the script supervisor, a woman from wardrobe and someone from production design. We all watched the last take's playback and I noticed the crew only focused on their particular contribution. The wardrobe woman was happy the stain she'd baby-wiped wasn't picking up on camera. The scripty focused on whether the words were all there and said in the right order. The person from production design focused on the set. Only the director was actually watching the scene, and he might be the type who focuses on lenses and lighting. Maybe if actors knew how few people were paying attention to their work while we were shooting, they'd feel more free.

I was thrilled to find Charlie's new entrance-to-the-pool-hall song was The Meters' *Fire On The Bayou*. I liked that he'd paired me with local music. Patrick squeezed my hand during the big fight scene where I battled two guys with a pool cue. I wasn't sure if it was the action scene that was intense for him or the flirting between my character and Ra's. I'd known Ra since we started out together in the early 90's. It made no sense that he wasn't here watching our big moment together. And I hated that Clarence wasn't here to say he was happy he'd chosen me and tell everyone stories about me at the after-party we wouldn't be having.

My spine straightened when I heard those first plucked notes of Ann Peebles' *I Can't Stand the Rain*, signaling the start of my big, solo, Wing Chun training exercises scene. Closeups of my hands doing precise slicing-the-air and wrist-rolling fist movements matched the music's plucking. It was pretty darn cool. A Shaw Brothers-style zoom shot us back, exposing me as Charlie wearing a coral maxi-dress in a dojo. Charlie kicked her bare foot out exposing a slit in the dress all the way up her leg and a bunch of people in the crowd reacted, hooting and whistling. That made me feel happy, like I was doing a good job of entertaining and maybe even owning the scene.

A few people laughed and a couple clapped when I did the leg stretch with my toes straight into camera.

I whispered to Patrick, "That was the shot I came up with. He kept it!" I got an even bigger reaction when I did the matching kick-into-camera that Clarence had requested. He'd also kept my backbend that moved into a front toe-touch, and the split up the wall. When the scene ended, the whole audience cheered. I felt proud and hopeful that I was actually doing a good job.

When there were a lot of scenes in a row without Charlie, it was easier to relax into the movie. Sometimes I'd get carried away enough to forget I was even in what was clearly an award-worthy movie. I loved that the crowd would cheer a local with one line like they were the legendary Graham Paisley doing his Oscar clip. 7 Sisters had been the first big break for a lot of locals. I liked that we were celebrating our experience of this movie instead of clapping for the long-celebrated. We'd felt privileged to work with the amazing cast and crew, but because of Isaac – this night was ours.

A few of my scenes were cut, but I tried not to let it ache when I saw how many other amazing scenes had been cut from much bigger names. The big reveal scene seemed to catch a lot of the audience by surprise. Many of them had never seen the script. I started to get excited for the final fight scene in Dutch Alley. It was thrilling – explosions, horse tricks, fencing, boxing, a chainsaw fight, gymnastics and my Hapkido moves.

When Hiroto came at Charlie with a sidekick and she scissored her legs, diving feet first between his legs, the theatre went bananas. As the fight ended, Charlie stood over her defeated prey and smirked,

"Tell Daddy hey." Then she smashed her wedge heel into his face/the camera. Lots of people laughed or exclaimed and I wondered if the humor would translate in other cultures. Heck, I wasn't even positive it would translate outside of this room full of friends and coworkers.

Everyone cheered victoriously at the end. I happy-cried, overwhelmed with a feeling of accomplishment and togetherness. Funky twangs introduced Sisters Love confronting us with *Ha Ha Ha*, a sexy, cool 1970 release about rising above misery but used as a groovy, she-who-laughs-last type of song. The actors credits were paired with short clips that froze into comic-book-like renderings next to our names. The seven sisters were first. There was a smattering of applause for the first five, then a roar as my clip filled the screen. It was from the pool hall fight where Charlie was wearing a suede miniskirt and white go-go boots, twirling a cue stick like a parade baton. As she lunged forward for a hit, the frame froze and became a fierce-faced graphic rendering next to my name. I wanted to frame it and hang it on a wall.

We sat through every last credit, clapping for lighting guys, set painters and production assistants. Patrick and I screamed for Wendy, of course. The genial guy who held all of our cell phones and other electronics got huge applause. He was clearly beloved. The whole experience felt intimate. No press and no producers, directors and stars also meant no pressure. It was kind of nice, like a cast and crew screening but without people inviting their agents.

Patrick took a picture of me standing next to the

poster as we exited into a sea of hugging, celebratory people. My name wasn't on the one-sheet but Charlie was one of the seven full-body silhouettes posing between the title and "A Clarence Pool Picture."

They'd canceled the afterparty and people were debating which bar to invade. Some wanted to stay close by, some voted to return to a bar they'd frequented when Clarence was here. I was surprised to find John Schneider in the crowd. We hugged and I introduced him to Patrick.

They shook hands then John focused on me and laughed. "Tell Daddy hey! That was awesome. You were great. This is gonna be great for you."

"You think so? It's not a huge part and it's a pretty star-packed movie."

He chuckled. "Come on. It's a Clarence Pool movie. You already know the kind of impact that can have."

I smiled. "Yeah, but I'm stayin' put. Not sure the opportunity'll translate down here."

He nodded. "Fair. You're not going back to L.A.?"

"Been there, done that. But you already know the kind of impact a place like this can have."

He laughed, then hugged and smiled his way toward his car. Patrick smiled. "That was Bo Duke."

"Yeah, I never saw the show."

He laughed. "I had the lunch box."

"You did?"

"Yeah, I loved *Dukes of Hazard*."

It was kind of cute seeing Patrick as a fan. He was always so cool around my fancy friends. I'd finally found one that tapped into that childhood fandom – the fandom of someone free of cynicism, someone unclear on the line between fantasy and reality. It seemed sweet somehow, like I was seeing the boy inside my man.

It would've been fun joining everyone for the bar invasion but I was ready to call it. "You wanna go?"

Patrick looked surprised and a little sympathetic. "You don't want to go to the bar? I'm sure all those people wanna tell you how great you were."

"You think I was great?"

He laughed. "You were amazing. But you already know I don't have it in me to tell you all the stuff they will. And they're not haunted by the memory of you coming home and strapping ice on yourself head to toe for months."

I laughed. "I'm good. Seriously. I feel good about all of it. I'll admit I want to hear more about what you thought of everything, but I'm good with going home. Besides, I can't compete with the cell phone guy."

Patrick hugged me and led me across the street. "True. But did you notice everyone saying 'tell Daddy hey' as we were leaving the theatre?"

"Seriously? I have a tag line?" Though I had to wonder if audiences that weren't filled with my neighbors, friends and coworkers would react the same way, I kind of liked that idea. Tell Daddy hey. I could live with strangers saying that to me for a few years.

Chapter 19

We'd stayed in most of the weekend watching movies and making puzzles while the giant party played out day and night outside. When we'd sit on the stoop and watch the wacky world go by, inevitably someone would ask how we dealt with the chaos and noise. We always answered the same, "No one ever moved to the French Quarter for the peace and quiet." And the city was in some ways so well-planned. Most of our bedrooms were far from the noise, totally insulated in the center of the city block.

As we wandered the crowded Quarter in search of food, I tried not to be irritated that the streets were packed with travelers yet no one made it to our premiere. I wanted to let the whole thing go, but it felt like a rip-off or a lie. I watched two men holding hands in front of us and wondered if they were allowed to do that at home. Southern Decadence was about partying and costumes and actual decadence, but it was also about feeling safe holding hands in front of a restaurant, checking out a menu. Just like Patrick and I were doing next to them – and took for granted.

Many of the restaurants in the city had to get rid of their food during the power outage and deliveries were disrupted, so most of them had very limited menus. Some could print them out but most didn't, which led to a long ordering process.

I started the game. "Is the Sirloin Stuffed Potato as good as it reads?"

Our exhausted waitress managed a smile. "We don't have beef."

"Oh, okay. How about a bowl of chili."

She chuckled. "We really don't have any beef."

I laughed. "Right. How about the chicken tortilla soup?"

"No chicken tortilla soup."

"Okay. Do you have..."

We ended up with a sausage and rice dish and a plate of potato skins. Sitting in air conditioning and filling my belly, I wondered how less fortunate areas of the city were managing. Though it felt strange to dance in the streets while people were suffering, tourism supported this city and no good could come from being a party pooper. The people who made it to Decadence had to reschedule flights or find open, un-submerged highways to get to town – and they looked forward to filling the city's coffers just when we needed it. Besides, folks here were used to celebrating life on its own terms - funerals and all.

There were people on our stoop waiting for the parade when we got back to the house. We told them they could stay, but they moved on just as Robert walked up waving. "Hey! Happy Decadence."

"Happy Decadence."

Robert pushed through the crowds of Decadence-goers and locals out for a fun parade after spending days fixing whatever was broken and cleaning what was filthy. Maybe it was odd to bring kids, but children here were used to seeing men in glitter and dresses for any number of reasons. We all needed something sparkly to take our minds off broken things and mud.

Robert bounded up the stairs and hugged me. "I have to tell you. I did it!"

Patrick peeked out and invited us inside for beverages. We followed him in, Robert nearly bubbling-over to tell his story and me dying to hear it as Patrick offered beers, Cokes and a smattering of liquors left over from previous guests. As Patrick started to lead us back out, I could take it no more. "What happened?"

We all stopped in the living room as Robert acted out his big moment. "I called the Garden District police after I got your text and asked them to drive by my house, told them I'd had a report of a possible intruder. Thank you for that, by the way."

I smiled and sat, pulling Patrick onto the couch beside me.

Robert continued with his regaling. "The tour was almost over when you texted so I wrapped things up and the police called when I was just a few blocks from home. Officer Signal said they'd apprehended someone and was I in the area? I pull up just as they're taking Emma out of the house in handcuffs."

My mouth dropped. "Are you serious?" That had to be difficult for him. As much as she'd put him through, he still seemed blinded by his feelings for Emma no matter what we uncovered. "I like Officer Signal. He's reasonable."

Robert was smiling. He was nearly the cat who ate the proverbial canary. "Officer Signal was holding her by the elbow like in a perp walk and I tried to see her the way he saw her."

"Really? Robert, that's amazing. What'd you see?"

He looked at Patrick then back to me. "I saw an unbalanced woman who broke into her ex's house to torment him."

Patrick nodded. "Repeatedly."

I couldn't help but feel like I'd helped, and I always liked that feeling. Robert hadn't just caught the "bad guy," he seemed to finally be moving past their relationship. "Did you say anything? Did she?"

Robert was nearly giddy. "She said, 'Tell them you gave me the key. Tell them we're friends.'"

"Ew, really?"

He nodded then stood warrior-like for his finale. "Officer Signal asks do I know her and I said, 'We're not friends. And I took the key to my house back years ago. She must've copied it behind my back.' Then I said, 'Does that show some sort of premeditation?'"

I gasped. "You didn't."

"I did." He thrust his arm into the air. "J'accuse!" My mom did that sometimes. What an odd thing to have in common. "They caught her red-handed. You should read the report. She was inside my family home with a bag full of tools and rigs. She was just gonna keep doing it. It didn't even seem to occur to her that I'd put my foot down in any way."

Patrick chuckled. "She knows now."

I wasn't done yet. "Did she say why she did it?"

"No, but she kept saying, 'Tell them, tell them it was your idea.'"

"What was your idea? The haunting? Was it?"

Robert cocked his head. "No. I get it now, she's

not right in the head. She used to say if she lived in a haunted house, she'd love telling the story. She said I was lucky to be the Lonely Boy."

Was he still stuck on her? "Lucky? So, she was helping?"

"No, she was unbalanced."

Robert was so clear-headed. I was always finding new ways acting techniques could be useful in the offstage world. I jumped up and gave him a hug. "I'm so glad you didn't try to save her. That had to be hard but you must feel better."

"It's not just that the house doesn't do weird things anymore, it's like I'm... stronger? That's not the right word."

Patrick stood to greet Margie on the stoop. "Yeah it is. It can take a lot to let someone go, even if they're nothin' but trouble." Patrick and I had both walked some miles in those shoes.

We spilled out onto the stoop and exchanged hugs with Margie as the wailing woman down the street came out of her house in a fitted polkadot dress, pink with white dots. I hit Patrick's arm. "There she goes."

Patrick looked up at the polka-dotted woman staggering down her steps, then at me. "Only a matter of time before she's wailing in the streets."

Margie and Robert turned to see the object of our attention. Robert turned back almost immediately. "Miss Lucille? Tragic. Married her college sweetheart, moved into the city like they'd always talked about. Money, youth, love, all of it. Then he died."

My chest collapsed. It was my habit to feel others' feelings, but her pain was too heavy a load to carry.

After battling my fears that Patrick was just another L.A.-type player, I'd finally let him fill my heart and my life. I couldn't let myself imagine losing Patrick to death. I had no curiosity. I didn't want to know how her husband had died or how long they'd had together before his passing. I didn't want any specifics for my imagination to hang onto and obsess over every time I heard her wailing. Maybe it was better that I'd spent so much of my youth alone, maybe it meant I'd get to grow old with the best man I'd ever met. It certainly meant I rarely took him or us for granted. And someday soon, we would marry.

It was my habit to focus on questions and details. I could go down mental wormholes dissecting and positing. But Ashley the Traffic Tranny was blowing her whistle, leading the parade past us. The city was demanding that I live in the moment. Living in the moment was pretty much the motto of method acting. It meant letting experiences wash over you in real time. It meant reacting instinctively from a place of truth. In L.A., I'd gotten better at doing that in front of a camera than in life. It felt unsafe to fully be myself in L.A. Like the sparkly, beaded people parading past, I felt safe here. I felt like I could let my busy brain rest and just enjoy stuff.

Then I lifted my camera to snap photos for my blog. Maybe I would always be driven to observe the life I was living in some way.

There were fantastical drag queens in costumes that were part disco dress, part chandelier. One fishnetted queen held a sign with a joke about being "blown by Isaac." It was clear the hurricane had impacted attendance when the parade only took twenty minutes to pass. About a dozen of my pink, glittery Pussyfooter sisters danced by and a few waved. Caroline was wearing her spectacular feathered-mohawk headdress. I waved and blew kisses to her, Christine and my sponsor, Sabine. It was fun knowing so many people in a parade. And next Mardi Gras, I'd be one of those Pussyfooters strutting St. Charles while appreciative neighbors and visitors cheered on the Pink Army.

As an actor, I'd gotten to live pieces of many people's lives. I'd walked imaginary miles in the shoes of scientists, strippers, mothers and mistresses. I'd even gotten to be a southern-belle, multi-discipline martial artist with six sisters. It could be fascinating at times, but lately the soundtrack in my head often found its way back to *Rocky Horror Picture Show*'s climactic *Don't Dream It, Be It*. I was a Pussyfooter. I was becoming part of the culture I'd tried to capture in my blog.

Though it'd started as an anonymous journal to keep my friends in L.A. with me when I first moved to New Orleans, readers in over a hundred countries were now living vicariously through my musings, photos and videos. As parade season revved up, I could report from the inside. I knew the blogging was just another way to avoid total immersion in relaxed fun, but I'd long ago accepted my brain's voracious appetite for activity.

Even with the chandelier safely uptown, my thoughts still tugged at the new questions I had about our family heritage. I'd never put much stock into the idea that ancestors could affect the type of person you became, but I'd always been the kind of person who could leap into the unknown – and I could do it alone. I was made of strong stuff. I was born of rebel heart-followers. But I couldn't imagine being Lily at a time when women couldn't even own property in most states, and finding it within myself to run away from everything I knew and all those creature comforts for love of the overseer. Daisy and Bird married when it wasn't even their right. These were bold women and daring men. As were my parents. Who were apparently cousins of some sort. It was a lot to absorb. Slaves and slave owners. Sometimes I hated thinking about it. Just like the magnificent plantations peppering our region, much of the beauty and romance was borne of unspeakable ugliness.

Would the chandelier rest now that I knew I was born of both sides of the slavery equation? Was that the secret Sassy's family was meant to protect? Maybe the reason Sassy never told the twins was because the world had changed. Maybe she thought it would be okay if the story was revealed. But she'd been so adamant about the twins keeping the chandelier hung, hiding the initials and Wells plantation symbol. Could there be more to the secret? Was it an entirely different secret? Did Sassy even know about my dad's family? Why would she? Maybe that wasn't the secret at all.

A group of men in shiny purple Mylar fringe skirts and open silver vests walked by carrying DIY scepters. Fireworks-like sprays of silver rose from their heads. Sashaying behind them, a drag queen wearing a magenta wig sent my brain back to *Rocky Horror*. Don't dream it, be it. The procession of technicolor paraders was far more vivid and joyful than the manufactured euphoria of the ballroom scene in the movie. Dreams were wonderful but life was actual. I wanted to make sure I lived mine like I understood that this was not the dress rehearsal, this was my one and only life. Maybe I was like Lily, Leonard, Daisy and Bird. One thing was certain – I existed because they were willing to follow their hearts and leap into the unknown.

I was hoping the call with Miss Catherine, the family trees and Tate's research would make me feel settled somehow, like I finally saw things clearly. But I felt more driven than ever to know more about the people who'd paved the way for my coming into being. Why did my family give Mama Eunoe the chandelier? And what about Mama Heck's diamond ring? Did it have a story? Had it been Mama Eunoe's as well? Was it originally Lily's or Daisy's? Or their mother's? Had Lily and Daisy stolen the treasures? Or were they secreted to the girls by a soft-hearted parent?

These were the worst kinds of questions. These were the questions that eluded answering without a witness account or personal letters. These were the questions that would nag at me, yanking me out of the unfolding now and into the unknowable past.

Could I find out more about Daisy leaving Texas and marrying Bird? Maybe there were more Cane River documents. Maybe Dad's sister, Carol, would remember something if we told her the story of Bird and Birdie being listed as Creole and the plantation burning. I didn't want my search for answers to end.

And I still felt irresponsible being in charge of a family secret I wasn't sure I'd uncovered. I was supposed to be The Protector and I wasn't even sure what I was protecting. How could I know if I was living up to the task?

Patrick and Robert went in for another round of beers as the last of the procession passed and the street filled with parade-goers looking for a party.

I watched Margie swaying her hips to a passing boom box. She laughed at one of the more clever costumes and I realized the questions would have to wait. I'd answered plenty of questions for Robert and deserved a brain-cation.

The man I'd waited a lifetime for was inside wearing a plastic tiara he'd caught, and laughing with our new friend. The partiers in the street were living life without bothering to question it or record it, save the occasional selfie.

Anaïs Nin said, "We write to taste life twice." I'd always loved that quote. It made me feel like there was something noble in my nostalgia. But the second time we tasted life was just the movie of the first time, the retelling. I wanted to make sure I was living a life worth retelling.

I tucked my camera inside the door and joined Margie on the stoop. We danced and laughed and pointed out pretty wigs and glittery heels – and I let all of it go unrecorded.

APPENDIX

These people and places mentioned in the book are real and open for business as of this publishing. For more information on anything mentioned in this book, use the search tool in LAtoNOLA (latonola.com), the blog upon which many of the book's recollections are based.

Armstrong Park
http://www.pufap.org/index.html

Belladonna
http://belladonnadayspa.com

Bryan Batt
http://www.bryanbatt.com

Bucktown All-Stars
http://bucktownallstars.com

Camellia Grill – the French Quarter location has ended its run.
Visit the original Uptown location.
https://en.wikipedia.org/wiki/Camellia_Grill

Commander's Palace
https://www.commanderspalace.com

Dancing Man 504
https://www.facebook.com/Dancing-Man-504-239176338346/

Dreamy Weenies – has ended its run.

Festigals
http://www.festigals.org

Gambit Weekly
https://www.bestofneworleans.com

Garden District Book Shop
http://www.gardendistrictbookshop.com

Steve Gleason/Team Gleason
http://www.teamgleason.org

Hubig's Pies – has ended its run.

Lisa Iacono
https://www.lisaiacono.com

Lafayette Cemetery #1
http://www.saveourcemeteries.org/lafayette-cemetery-no-1/

M.S. Rau Antiques
https://www.rauantiques.com

Matassa's Market
https://www.matassas.com

May Baily's Place
http://www.dauphineorleans.com/nightlife

Mia's Balcony – has ended its run.

Christine Miller – Two Chicks Walking Tours
http://www.twochickswalkingtours.com

Eric Paulsen, WWLTV
https://buff.ly/2H9jgoA

Margie Perez
https://www.facebook.com/MargiePerezSings

Prytania Theatre
https://www.theprytania.com

The Pussyfooters
http://www.pussyfooters.org

Red Dress Run
http://www.noh3.com

Ruby Slipper Cafe
https://www.therubyslippercafe.net

The New Orleans Saints
http://www.neworleanssaints.com

St. Louis Cemetery #1
http://www.saveourcemeteries.org/st-louis-cemetery-no-1/

John Schneider Studios
https://www.johnschneiderstudios.com

Snowizard
http://www.snowizardsnoballshop.com/index-main.php

SoBou
https://www.sobounola.com

The Soul Rebels
http://thesoulrebels.com

Southern Decadence
http://www.southerndecadence.net

Superdome
http://www.mbsuperdome.com

Trashy Diva
http://www.trashydiva.com

Treme Brass Band
https://www.facebook.com/TremeBrassBand/

ABOUT THE AUTHOR

Best known for her role as Leonardo DiCaprio's sister in Quentin Tarantino's *Django Unchained*, Laura Cayouette has acted in 45 films including *Now You See Me*, *Kill Bill* and *Enemy of the State*. Television appearances include *True Detective*, *Friends* and a recurring role on *Queen Sugar*.

Laura earned a Master's Degree in creative writing and English literature at the University of South Alabama where she was awarded Distinguished Alumni 2014. She currently resides in New Orleans.

Website: lauracayouette.com
Twitter: @KnowSmallParts
Facebook: http://bit.ly/1VxJIvr